TOO EMBARRASSED TO SING

BY
TANYA
HOLT

Published by The Singing Detective
First published in October 2021
ISBN 978-1-7398126-1-4

Editor: Samantha Cook
Book cover & design: General Dynamic, www.generaldynamic.studio

For permission requests contact: press@thesingingdetective.com

www.tooembarrassedtosing.com

Contents

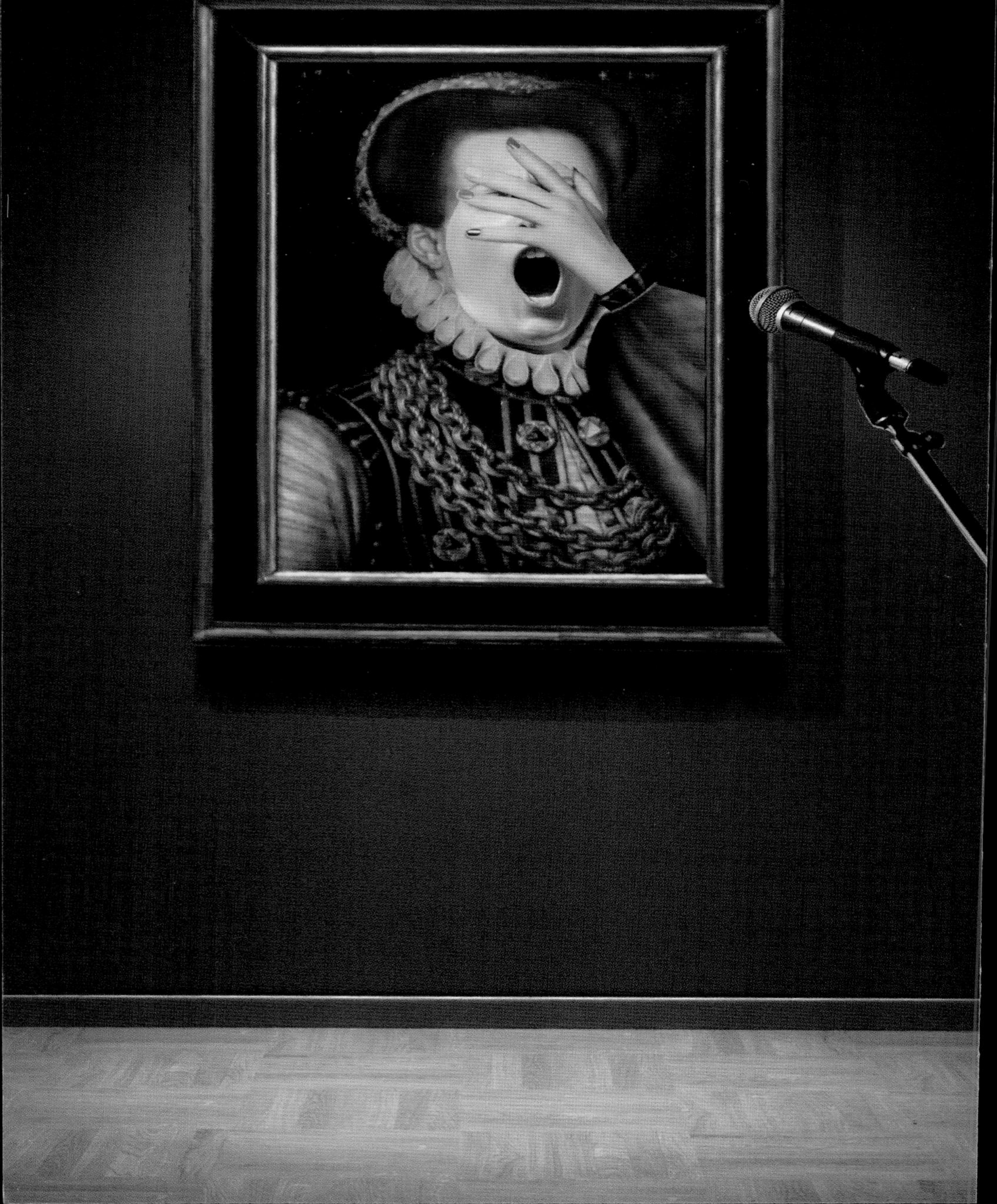

Introduction

Singing can induce such extreme levels of self-criticism and embarrassment that it's a wonder anyone dares to do it, even in their own company

At the end of her lesson, Vera Weghmann slipped her feet back into her red stilettos and told me a story.

She vividly described how she had been at a party and when the crowd began to sing, rather than breaking out in a cold sweat of self-consciousness, as she would have done a few weeks earlier, she found herself wanting to join in. This was the first time in her life that she had allowed herself to sing in company. An unforgettable moment of triumph.

The joy of the retelling of this experience had us both whimpering like schoolgirls who had just discovered that our teenage crush crushed us back. More pragmatically, it reminded me of why I had felt the need to write Too Embarrassed to Sing.

If, like Vera once was, you are embarrassed or even ashamed to open your mouth to sing in company, take some comfort in knowing that there are armies of people who feel exactly the same way. As a singer and singing teacher, I regularly have to defend myself against individuals who want me to know, almost as a badge of honour, that they can't sing or have a 'dreadful voice' and are beyond saving. (Depressingly, these self-evaluations are often the result of stinging criticisms received as children.) As you can imagine, my firm response is to tell these people that it is not so much that they 'can't', but that they 'have never learned to' sing. I won't budge on this. I have witnessed countless times, at first hand, the miracle of people who couldn't hit a single note in tune transform into self-confident singers with 'good' voices.

There is a prevailing myth that some people are born with beautiful voices and others are not. This is simply not true; a beautiful sounding voice is the consequence of a singer having learned, formally or instinctively, how to use the muscles of their throat, mouth and lips to 'shape' their sound. The outcome of singing with a tight jaw or with tension in your tongue, both of which are extremely common, is likely to be described as 'not very good' or less politely, 'a bad voice'. Sadly, these correctible mistakes can define a person's relationship with their singing voice for life.

Over the next chapters you will discover how good posture and breath control can make singing feel – and sound – easy. You might be amazed by how much control you can have over the quality of your voice just by dropping your jaw or by changing the shape of your lips. Learning how to engage your core muscles will make your breath last much longer and help keep you in tune, and by experimenting with the sense of space in your throat you will add layers of beautiful harmonics to your voice.

It will become quickly obvious that singing is largely a muscular activity and as we – generally – share the same anatomy, it stands to reason that every human being who can speak should also be able to sing. It's also worth noting that there are no muscles specifically or exclusively designed for singing.

Most of the muscle sets we need in order to sing cannot be triggered in isolation, nor are they under conscious control, so in this book I will

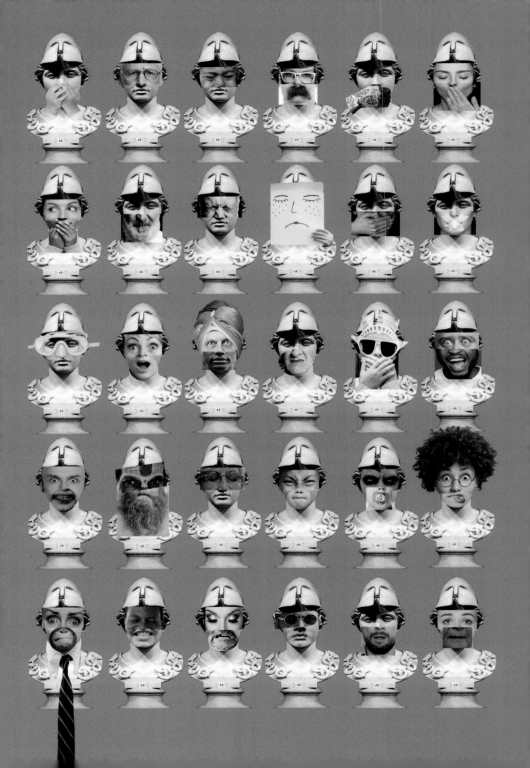

SPOT
THE
DIFFERENCE

TAB.
XXVI.
TAB.
XXVI.

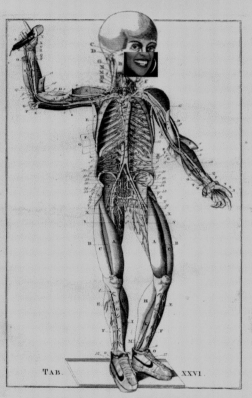

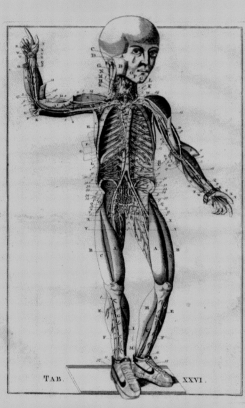

How many anatomical differences can you spot between the singer and the non-singer?

Answer: none

teach you how to use a few simple and accessible triggers. For example, imagining sniffing a beautifully fragranced flower will activate the many muscles of the face and the roof of the mouth and can have a brightening effect on the quality of the sound you make. Complain about something, on the other hand, and you will immediately feel your throat change shape, which can prepare you for certain singing tasks in your higher ranges. My students squeeze the juice out of make-believe oranges in their armpits to activate their back muscles to help with singing high notes and long phrases. These actions, and their benefits, are all easily attainable with practice.

> Every sung sound is the consequence of activating muscles designed to do things you are already doing without even thinking about it

It really does take the most minimal level of curiosity and effort for anyone to be able to tap into their vocal potential – and I do mean anyone, at any stage and any age. I would shout it from the rooftops, if shouting wasn't so bad for the voice, so instead, I'd like to tell you the story of what motivated me to write this book.

About twelve years ago my parents gave me a little orange tree as a birthday present; a surprising choice, perhaps, in view of my historical reputation for botanical negligence. True to form, my total lack of care quickly reduced the tree to tumbleweed. When I moved house, ten years later, I felt obliged to take the lifeless tree with me and positioned it in a hidden spot in my newly planted garden. Quite unlike my former self, I was now precious about my new plants and took the utmost care of them, with regular watering, weeding and feeding – and meanwhile, I would occasionally remember to throw some plant food and water over the little orange tree. One day, an infestation on my apple tree required an emergency spraying and, not wanting to take any chances, I sprayed everything in sight – including the neglected orange tree. It will probably be no surprise to hear that after a few weeks of almost inadvertent care, it began to produce beautiful, waxy leaves and is now bearing fruit. For ten years I had neglected it, never bothering to understand its needs, and consequently I got the tree I deserved. It now gives me endless joy – and oranges. Though it might sound somewhat naive, I was genuinely amazed by how little it took to transform its fortunes.

> You don't need to have any music theory, previous knowledge, or a Steinway in your front room to get the most out of this book

This experience provoked an intense moment of epiphany in me: I wanted to write a persuasive and practical guide for all those people who would love to be able to sing but have unwittingly consigned themselves to the metaphorical sunless spot of the garden. You absolutely can cultivate your singing voice if you want to.

I have arranged the chapters to fit a linear style of learning, so you're more likely to get the full benefit of it by reading it in order, from cover to cover to start with, and then by dipping into it for specifics. I have covered the 'non-negotiables' (also known as technique) – posture, breathing and shaping the vocal tract – along with ideas on artistry and performance, and there's a chapter on how to listen and learn from other artists.

You will find images and tips throughout to help you get to grips with the trickier technical elements, and gentle reminders to keep the vital requirements of good singing in the forefront of your mind. As we can't see inside our bodies, learning to sing relies on sensations and trigger images, which, it turns out, can be quite a challenge to illustrate. I made the bold decision (I am not a visual artist) to create collages for this purpose. I hope you find them helpful and entertaining as well as memorable enough to keep in mind while singing.

I have enjoyed thinking about who you are as I write and I have imagined you as the collective faces, voices and personalities of all those people who have passed through my teaching studio. If we were in the room together I would remind you to be patient with yourself, to practise little and often and not to be put off when you have a setback. With commitment and this book as your guide, there will come a moment when you experience the unmistakable sensation of setting your voice free. It will feel wonderful. Ask Vera.

I feel excited for you!

Tanya

CHAPTER

ONE

THE

MYTH

OF

TALENT

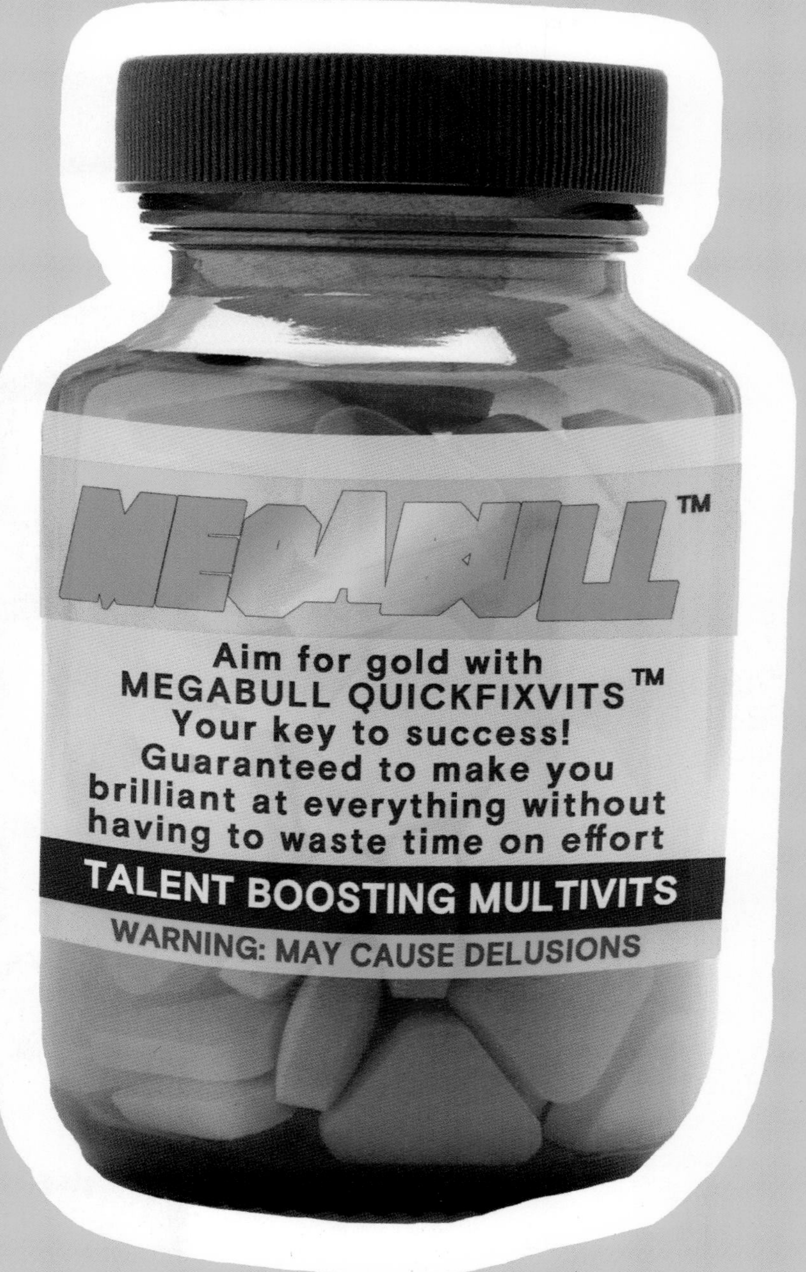
MEGABULL™
Aim for gold with
MEGABULL QUICKFIXVITS™
Your key to success!
Guaranteed to make you
brilliant at everything without
having to waste time on effort
TALENT BOOSTING MULTIVITS
WARNING: MAY CAUSE DELUSIONS

The myth of talent

In the mouths of the wrong people, words like 'talent' or 'natural ability' can be so disempowering; the only way to master a skill is to learn and practise

We are too quick to judge ourselves and others, often by making unfavourable comparisons with more experienced singers. If you are expecting to sing 'Nessun Dorma' as beautifully as Pavarotti, but without any kind of wherewithal, you will be disappointed. Imagine trying to win the Grand National when you've never so much as ridden a donkey in Skegness. Lots of people give up at the first hurdle, convinced that Mother Nature is having a joke at their expense.

The rise in the popularity of TV talent shows has made singing something of a spectator sport and has generated all kinds of myths about the essence of talent. Let me assure you that, however much the contestants on our screens are presented as 'ordinary', we are actually looking at people who have already invested in themselves, even if that investment isn't recognised in a formalised way. The romantic notion that these overnight sensations have simply been born with an incredible and surprising ability makes for inspirational viewing, but it also suggests that true talent is somehow innate, and that training (formal or self-taught) is for those with a lesser gift.

The truth is that training – guided learning and practice – is essential for anyone who wants to sing well. Britain's Got Talent winner Paul Potts (whose job as a mobile phone salesman was mercilessly exploited to make his meteoric rise to fame seem even more fantastic) is quite right to be irritated by the media's insistence that he was somehow cheating when it was 'discovered' that he had had singing lessons. He won the competition precisely because he had devoted himself to learning and practising. Even navel-gazing singer-songwriters with no performing experience are likely to have spent many hundreds of hours 'self-teaching' in their bedrooms, watching YouTube videos and recording themselves.

And there are other factors at play when it comes to the myth of natural talent. Hugely successful commercial singers who don't have any kind of obvious formal training will have worked hard on developing their skills and are likely to be performing material written specifically for their voices and for their level of ability, showcasing them at their best. Auto-Tune and other technologies can also radically enhance the quality of any performance, while theatrical showmanship or outstanding songwriting, rather than vocal expertise, can position artists favourably on a world stage.

Imagine trying to win the Grand National when you've never so much as ridden a donkey in Skegness

There can be any number of reasons, not often obvious, that account for why some people, despite having no previous experience, seem to be effortlessly good at singing. Don't compare yourself with these people and try not to be put off by what anyone else sounds like. While it might appear that some people are better than others at specific singing tasks, it doesn't mean that those others won't get it; it's just that they need to practise repeatedly until that task becomes second nature.

There are also all sorts of ways in which 'circumstance' can facilitate talent. Serena and Venus Williams are the daughters of tennis-playing parents, without whose passion and support they almost certainly would never have picked up a tennis racquet. There might be any number of potential Serena and Venus Williamses in the world who have simply never been exposed to a tennis-playing opportunity. What if their parents had been musicians or science teachers?

Similarly, our cultural landscape would look very different if Reg Dwight's grandmother hadn't owned the piano that would spark the young boy's interest in playing – and ultimately led to him becoming Elton John.

My school employed their first-ever dedicated singing teacher, Miss Brocklehurst, in response to the arrival of an exceptionally 'talented' ten-year old pupil (me). Much as I enjoyed this flattering status, I was actually displaying the results of five years spent in an unrelenting daily regime of religious singing in a Belgian convent. It was no wonder, with all those hours of practice, that I had developed great tone and stamina and demonstrated an impressive degree of musicality for my age. I absolutely loved singing and would make a concerted effort to be good at it. The school didn't consider the influence of this previous experience, preferring to take the view that my skill was 'miraculous'. My parents luxuriated in the sudden discovery of their daughter's extraordinary natural talent.

I always knew I wanted to be a singer. I didn't go to music college, but as a hardworking perfectionist with a love of singing, I determined to become as good as I possibly could be under my own steam. Years later, I'd get asked by post-show audiences where I had trained, but rather than be impressed by my unorthodox journey, the truth would generate palpable disappointment. No certificate? Perhaps she's not so good after all? In order to satisfy their need for my validation, I began to respond by telling them that I had, of course, trained at the 'Royal College' – or, for those wanting more detail, the Royal College of Musical Theatre and Cabaret in Burkina Faso.

When and where you start to learn and the route you take should have absolutely no bearing on how you are perceived as a singer. It is irrelevant. Your job as a singer, ultimately, is to engage your audience (even if it's just your mum or your own reflection) with the emotional narrative of the songs you are singing, and to do justice to the writers and composers.

In his excellent book Bounce: The myth of talent and the power of practice, Matthew Syed argues that outstanding performance is only achieved by practice. He references one particular study, undertaken by psychologist Anders Ericsson, which monitored the behaviour of a group of 'gifted' young musicians from the age of eight until they turned twenty. The study revealed, without exception, that after twelve years the outstanding performers were those who had practised many thousands of hours more than the others. The innate 'talent' shown in childhood had no bearing on whether that child developed into a exceptional artist.

Syed quotes Jack Nicklaus, the greatest golfer of all time: 'Nobody – but nobody – has ever become really proficient at golf without practice... It isn't so much a lack of talent; it's a lack of being able to repeat good shots consistently that frustrates most players. And the only answer to that is practice'.

CHAPTER
TWO

WHAT

IS

AND

ISN'T

SINGING

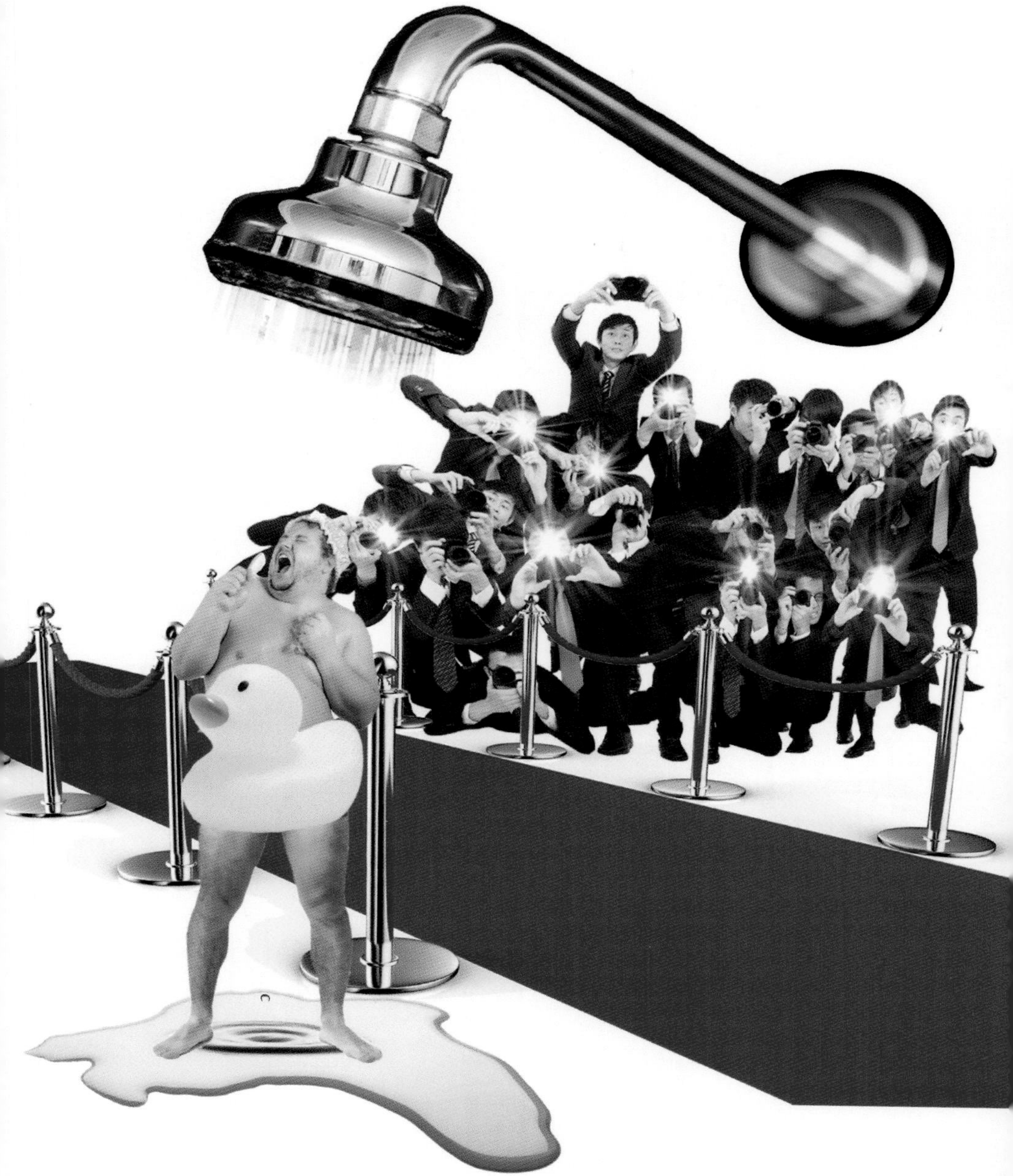

What is and isn't singing

Singing is a muscular activity
that uses your whole body

What isn't truly singing

Does this description fit you? Standing in the kitchen or sitting in the
car, radio blaring, singing joyfully and unabashedly along with Aretha,
Freddie or Ed. Singing so brilliantly. So effortlessly. Until you turn the
radio off and sing on your own. **Ouch.**

Or perhaps you are at a party when the music stops abruptly and
those high notes that you were hitting with such ease now possess an
uncannily feline quality and there's a definite hint of braying on the
lower ones. What was left of the melody of 'Say a Little Prayer' has
morphed, rather poetically, into the tune of 'Old MacDonald Had a
Farm'. I meet clients who sing along with their heroes and are baffled
that when they try it on their own they can no longer hit any of the
notes or stay in tune. The same thing happens to choir singers when
they are at home practising alone or attending online rehearsals.
Singing along to the radio, or in a choir surrounded by other singers,
relies almost completely on auditory feedback: in other words, you are
using your ears exclusively to match the pitch and rhythm of the song
being played. This isn't truly singing.

What is singing – physically

Using your ears is, of course, vitally important in singing, but less so
than you might think. Singing is a muscular activity that uses your

whole body; your voice is powered by your breath, and the way that you use that breath is controlled by your muscles. Without breath control your voice will wobble and sound untethered and the notes you make are likely to be out of tune and lack quality. You are also more likely to experience a sore throat. Additionally, the quality of the sound that you generate is heavily influenced by the micro-muscles of your throat and mouth. Your tongue alone possesses eight hardworking muscles that assist in chewing and swallowing and, more pertinently, are essential in forming words.

If you accept that singing is a physical act – like riding a bike, swimming or playing football – you have taken your first step in learning how to do it.

Let's transpose the scenario to a swimming pool and imagine that you are learning how to swim; you drop yourself into the water and discover pretty quickly that you can gain some level of buoyancy by kicking your legs and manipulating the water with your hands. Your swimming coach might put their hand under your back so you can feel the sensation of floating. You soon learn that by flattening your body in the water you can move faster, using less energy. You come to understand that by kicking your feet at the correct angle and by reaching out of the water with stretched arms and cupped hands you are working with the water to propel yourself forward. You need to master rhythmic breathing appropriate to the style of stroke and the distance you are going to swim.

None of these learned in isolation will allow you to actually swim, but once each has been practised, you will feel a beautiful moment of synchronicity when they start to work together and you find yourself powering effortlessly through the water. When you get it right, that's what singing feels like.

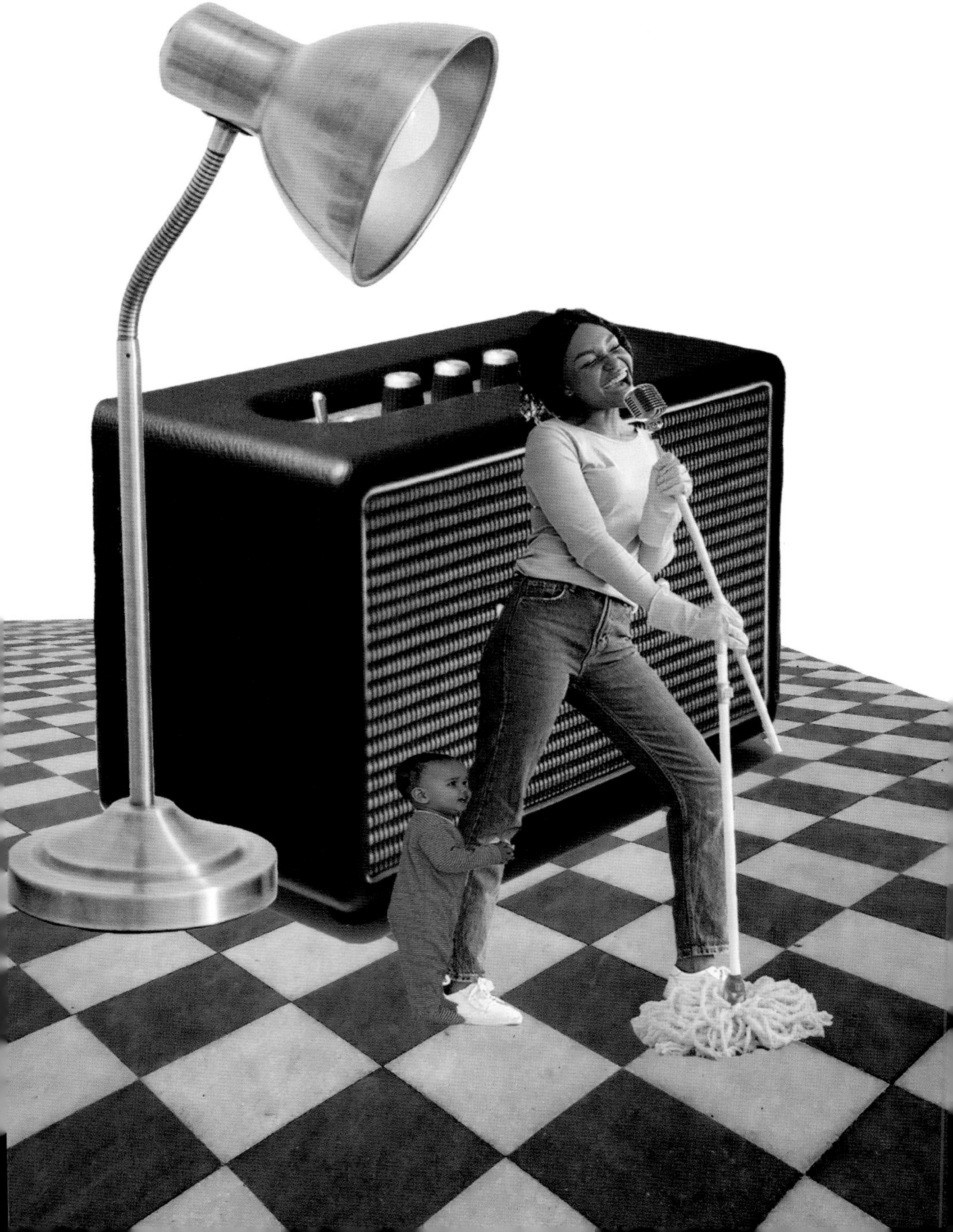

This same principle, of learning to feel when something is right, can be applied to the mastery of any physical skill; getting your balance on a bike, throwing a bowling ball or finding the 'sweet spot' in tennis. When you do eventually connect consciously with your voice for the first time, you will know it and it will be sensational.

What is singing – creatively and emotionally

Great performances are the result of a combination of technique and emotional imagination. Even the simplest of songs can be imbued with heartfelt poignancy if the singer puts effort into interpreting the text and recognising the emotional clues in the music. Singers have lots of useful tools to convey expression: dynamics (playing with volume), the use of different emotional responses in the throat (similar to changing your tone of voice when speaking) and smooth or rhythmic phrasing. Using these tools will ultimately enable you to deliver a performance that is authentic to you.

What is singing – technique

Preparing to sing is a bit like an artist preparing to apply paint to a canvas; irrespective of mixing expertise or brush wizardry, if the canvas is not properly stretched or primed, the artist is unlikely to be able to produce the quality of picture that their imagination aspires to.

Stabilising the body for singing with appropriate posture, controlling the airflow and shaping the vocal tract to produce good tone is collectively described as 'singing technique'. Every genre of singing has its own demands, but the essentials remain the same for all. Acquiring technique will build your self-confidence, improve your vocal health and allow you to consistently produce a good quality of sound.

CHAPTER THREE

SHAPING THE SOUND: DISCOVERING YOUR OWN VOICE

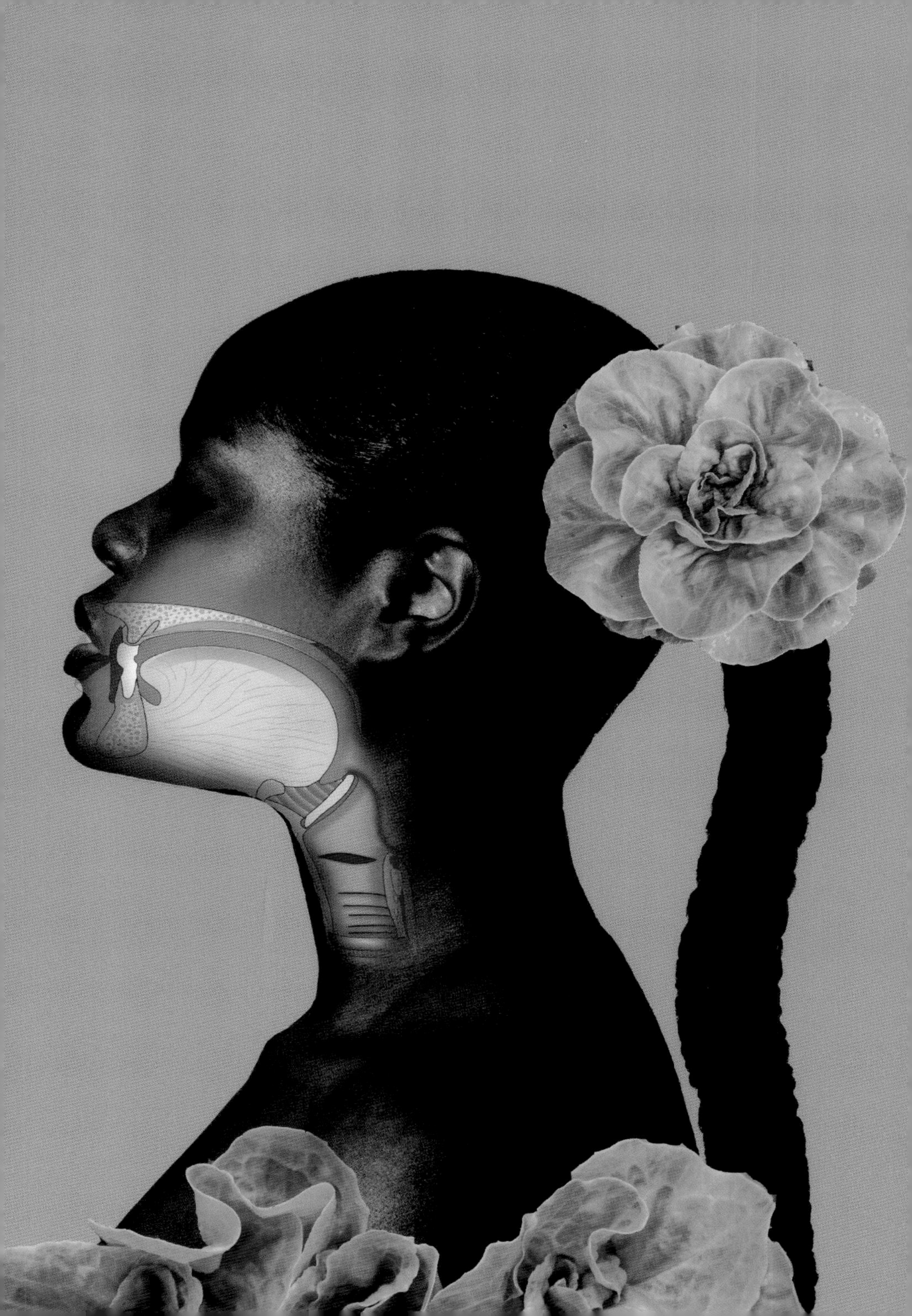

Shaping the sound: discovering your own voice

Unlike most musical instruments, which can be picked up and played straight away, the voice has to be built by the musician **before** it can be played

The main difference between the voice and other musical instruments is that man-made instruments have fixed sound-boosting airspaces and in human beings these airspaces are ever-changing. A sound-boosting airspace is the place where vibrating air is turned into the sound that we hear. It is the size, shape, texture and width of opening of these spaces that gives an instrument its signature sound.

Airspaces in musical instruments include the fixed space inside a guitar or violin and the open tube inside a flute or clarinet. In these instruments, the vibrations in the air are triggered by the buzzing of strings, or by breath being blown through a reed or across the top of a hole.

In humans, the sound-boosting space is the airway that starts in your throat and goes all the way up to your nostrils and lips. The vibrations in the air here are triggered by two vocal folds (also known as vocal cords) opening and closing extremely fast.

Large spaces generally boost the lower frequencies (like a bass drum or a tuba) and smaller spaces (imagine a piccolo) boost the higher ones. In humans, repositioning our tongues, jaws or lips immediately changes the size and shape of our airspaces, meaning that we can produce all kinds of fantastic sound combinations. This is what makes the human voice the most versatile (and the best), instrument of all. No bias, obviously!

These sound-generating airspaces are known as **resonating spaces** and in humans they are where the voice can be boosted in volume and quality.

Resonance – the system of shaping the airspace in order to boost particular harmonic frequencies – can be a baffling and misleading concept for singers, so I shall offer this rather unscientific but accessible explanation: resonance makes singing feel and sound easy. A lack of resonance can result in a voice sounding pushed, or dry, or breathy and quiet. You will know when you hear (or don't hear) resonance in other singers and when you feel it in your own body.

A resonating space must have an opening for the air to pass through so, contrary to popular belief, the sinuses and the chest cavity are not resonators; the feeling of buzzing in these areas while you are singing is sympathetic vibration, which occurs in the bony structures around your chest, head and face.

The vocal tract

Our 'corridor' of different, moveable, resonating airspaces is collectively called the **vocal tract**. Your vocal tract starts at the 'Adam's Apple' lump at the front of the throat, where the vocal folds are located. If you place your fingers gently on your throat at this point and speak or hum, you will feel your vocal folds vibrating. The vocal tract goes all the way up from that point to the nostrils and lips.

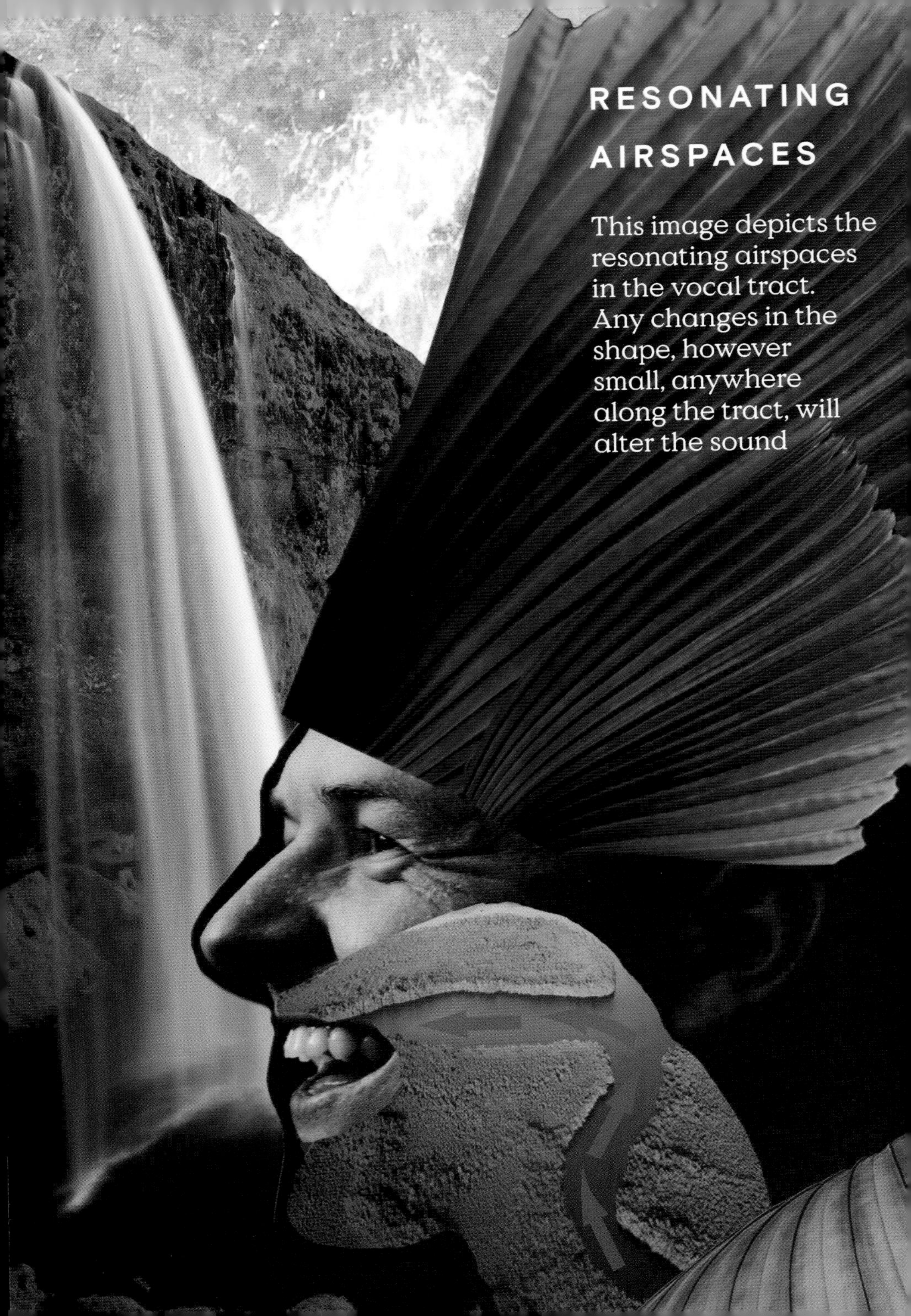

RESONATING AIRSPACES

This image depicts the resonating airspaces in the vocal tract. Any changes in the shape, however small, anywhere along the tract, will alter the sound

Your physical build will have an influence over the type of sound you produce. Long, wide vocal tracts are likely to give a darker, deeper quality of sound, while a short, thin vocal tract will enhance brighter, higher frequencies. The good news is that you can learn to adjust the length, width and shape of your vocal tract, building upon the starter kit you were born with.

The ability to change their resonating spaces is what enables singers to sound 'beautiful' and to successfully sing in a variety of styles. No one is born an opera singer or a heavy metal screamer – these are stylistic choices, ultimately achieved by learning how to control airflow and how to shape the vocal tract appropriately for that style.

> No one is born an opera singer
> or a heavy metal screamer –
> these are stylistic choices

You can start adjusting your resonating spaces straight away with a few simple movements. Pick a medium-range note and sing a sustained EE (like 'free'). Hold that EE and experiment with changing the quality of the sound by adjusting the shape of your lips and the opening of your jaw, and move the tongue up and down, and backward and forward, and flatten it. All of these adjustments will impact the sound in some way. Now sing a snippet of any song with your lips retracted into a broad smile and then sing the same phrase with a full pout. One will sound brighter and the other darker and richer.

Good quality sound requires air to be able to flow freely through any instrument's resonating spaces. The vocal tract has lots of muscles that allow you to squeeze, stretch and tighten all those resonating spaces, which can have fantastic outcomes but also means that it's possible to accidentally impede the airflow with a tense tongue or jaw. This is often what's happening to singers who think they have poor voices. We will be looking at this in more detail in Getting to know your vocal tract.

The difference between singing and speaking

In general, singing requires the jaw space to be wider than in speaking, and the back of the tongue to be in a more forward position, away from the back of the throat. This is in order to increase the resonating space in our throats, which is where our singing voices get the chance to 'ring'. However, you should be aware that a very wide jaw will reduce the size of this space. I will cover this later in Getting to know your vocal tract.

Try singing 'Happy Birthday' with your jaw and mouth positioned in a similar way to your speaking set-up. You should notice that this smaller mouth space produces a dull sound and the volume is limited. When you sing the higher notes, you may experience tension or discomfort at the back of your throat or in the base of your tongue.

Now try singing it again, but this time opening your jaw to a relaxed gap of about 0.5–1cm (about the width of a finger, depending on your build) between your upper and lower molars (the large grinding teeth at the back) and bring the back of your tongue forward, out of your throat, while still keeping the tip in your mouth, just behind your bottom front teeth. Imagine that you are just about to lick a lolly; the jaw drops open and the back of the tongue comes forward a little. Your mouth will naturally drop open as you do this. Now sing with this 'lolly' set-up. The sound should be significantly louder and richer.

In singing, it is the vowels that resonate, or 'ring', in the vocal tract. Consonants are formed with the articulators – the teeth, the lips and the tongue – and exist to make words out of vowels. Sing the word LOVE on any note, firstly with a short vowel and sustained VV followed by a sustained vowel and a short VV. You should get the picture pretty

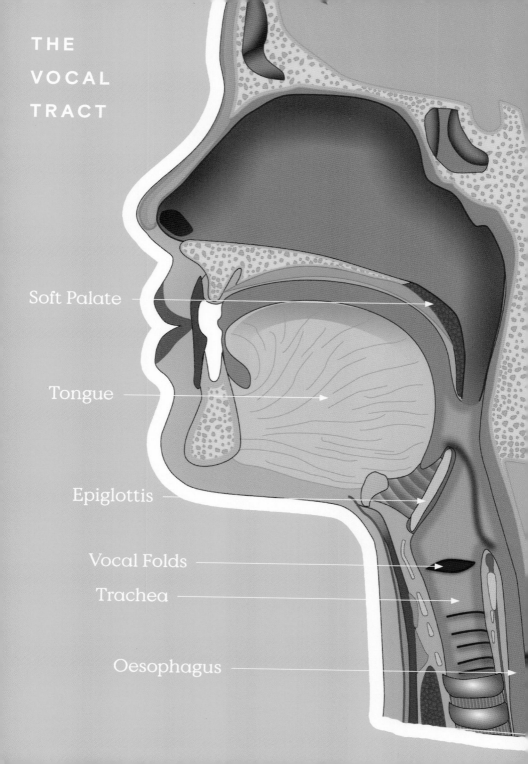

THE
VOCAL
TRACT

Soft Palate

Tongue

Epiglottis

Vocal Folds

Trachea

Oesophagus

quickly. In short: consonants are generally percussive and it is the vowels that create the ringing quality associated with singing.

Why you sing so well in the bathroom

Doesn't it feel fantastic to let rip with your favourite songs in the oh-so-flattering environment of the bathroom?

We have all experienced those fabulous Freddy-Mercury-in-a-shower-cap moments; that's because the sound that comes out of your mouth is also shaped by the space you are singing in. Think of the acoustics of a cave or tunnel. In a bathroom, the tiles and mirrors turn the room itself into a resonating space, providing a perfect system of hard surfaces on which the sound, once out of your mouth, can continue to bounce. Your sound stays in the air for longer as it pings between a multitude of different surfaces, becoming richer and louder. Meanwhile any flaws become blurry, making for a very satisfactory, if somewhat misleading, experience.

Concert halls, churches and older theatres are designed to allow sound to reverberate in a similar way, whereas recording studios often dampen the natural acoustics by cladding the booth or room with carpet and polystyrene in order to give the engineer complete control over the raw, 'dry' sound. They will artificially add 'bathroom' effects ('wet' sound) to the voice in post-production. Early in the COVID-19 pandemic you may have heard broadcasters describing their home-recording set-ups: cupboards, bunk beds and any small space, strewn with duvets and blankets to absorb the acoustic properties of the room and keep outside noise to a minimum. Every space, no matter how apparently quiet, has its own ambient sound.

If you have a tense jaw or unconsciously push your tongue towards the back of your throat while singing, you will produce the acoustic equivalent of a carpet-lined throat – ideal for performing songs from the Muppet Show, but not much else! (You will be surprised by how easy it is to do an impression of Kermit the Frog if you draw your tongue backward and speak in an American accent.)

Fortunately, it is possible to recreate the 'bathroom effect' in your vocal tract. To do this, you need to increase the sense of space in your throat and engage the walls of the resonating spaces. This is something I will explain in Getting to know your vocal tract, coming up shortly.

Discovering your sound library

In the 1980s, Jo Estill, an American singer turned pioneering vocal scientist, undertook groundbreaking research to assess how the position of the vocal tract changes with different styles of singing. Estill's legacy was a game-changer for singers and singing teachers; she replaced mystery with knowledge, encouraging a new generation of singers and actors to use scientific methods to achieve certain sounds and to better understand how to sing in a healthy way.

I was first introduced to this awareness exercise on an Estill training course and think it's a terrifically effective first step to understanding how to change your vocal tract by using imagination and emotion. I am not suggesting that you should be learning any particular style, just encouraging you to consciously recognise how versatile your voice already is.

Imagine that you are at a small child's birthday party and it is time to cut the cake and sing 'Happy Birthday'. Perform the song in the voice of each of the guests described below, experimenting with 'thinking and feeling' the appropriate emotion before you start singing:

1   A bored adult who sings almost as they might speak

2   An innocent young child who sings breathily and in a higher pitch

3   A playground bully just arrived from America

4   A flamboyant great aunt who is the leading light in the local amateur operatic society and wants everybody to know it!

5   A guest who has been missed off the party bag list and is rather upset, so consequently sings with a sob

If you are able to discern some differences in the sounds that you make as each 'guest', you will have successfully changed the shape of your vocal tract.

Now try singing a passage from a song you already know, in each of those same five settings. Sing a snippet of 'Happy Birthday' before you start on your own song, just to make sure that the vocal setting stays in place. Remember to establish the emotional connection first off, to help prepare your vocal tract. Great performers will use several different vocal settings in one song. Have fun!

CHAPTER FOUR

GETTING TO KNOW YOUR VOCAL TRACT

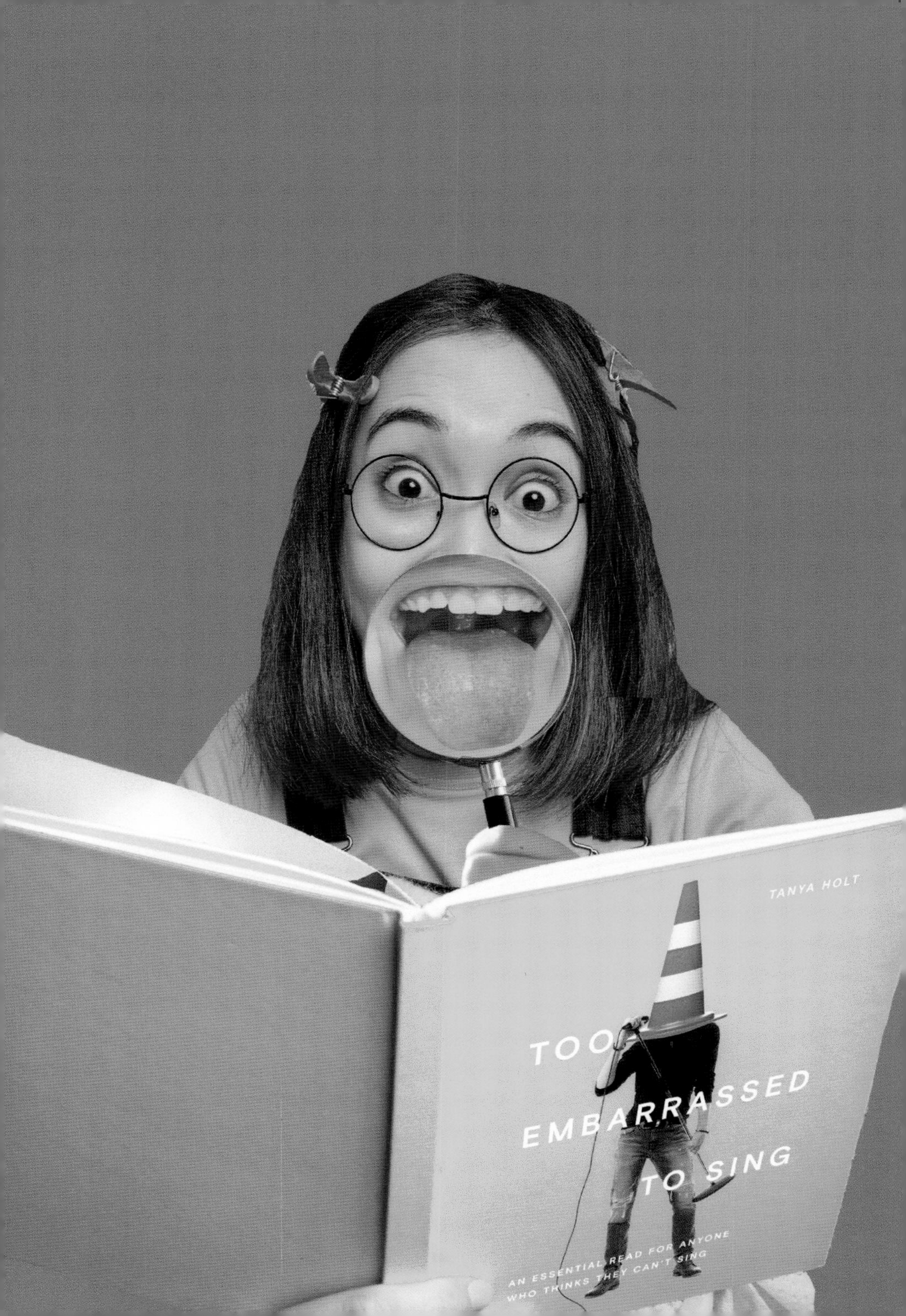
TANYA HOLT
TOO EMBARRASSED TO SING
AN ESSENTIAL READ FOR ANYONE WHO THINKS THEY CAN'T SING

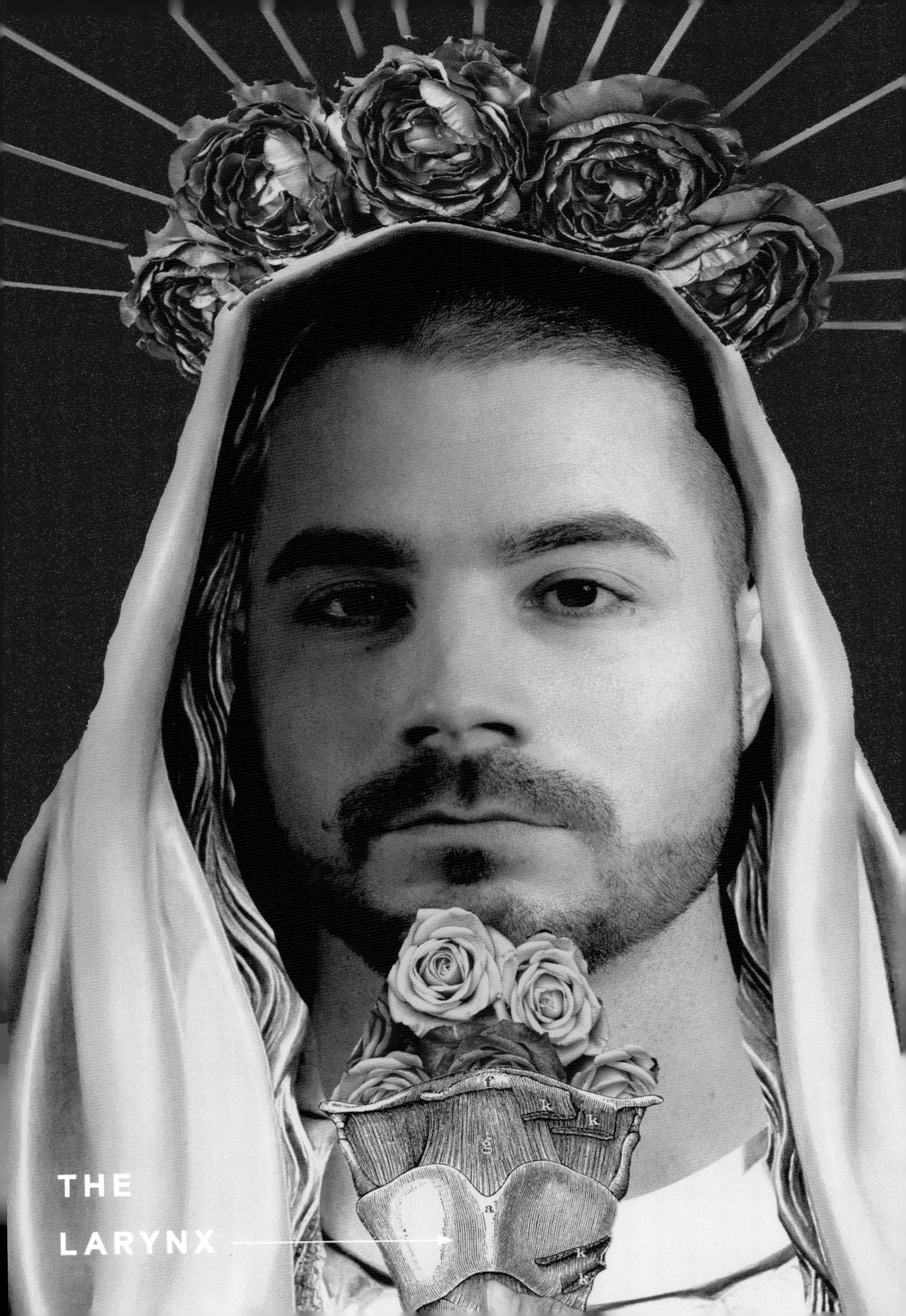
THE
LARYNX

Getting to know your vocal tract

You might be impressed by how quickly you can improve with relatively small changes

Getting familiar with the resonating spaces and main components of your vocal tract will help you to understand and visualise the sensations you feel during singing and allow you to make appropriate adjustments.

The larynx/voice box

The voice box, which is also called the larynx, is the part of the throat that we can see rising and falling, most noticeably when we swallow and yawn. It is made up of a protective tube of muscle and cartilage that houses the vocal folds (also called vocal cords). The Adam's Apple protrusion, which everyone has but is particularly prominent in men, provides protection for the vocal folds, which sit immediately behind it.

To feel the vibration of the vocal folds inside your larynx, try gently putting two fingers sideways across your Adam's Apple and then sing AH on any medium-pitched note. If you are struggling to find your Adam's Apple, run a finger from under your chin down the front of your throat and you will get to a point when you feel a definite bump. That's where you need to place your fingers. Now sing a very low Father Christmas "ho, ho, ho" and you should notice a sudden downward movement of the larynx. Conversely, a high-pitched giggle should

Back views: cartilaginous (l) & muscular (r)

d
c
c
a
a
b
d
p
p
o
n

f
k
k
g
a
k
k
h
i
b

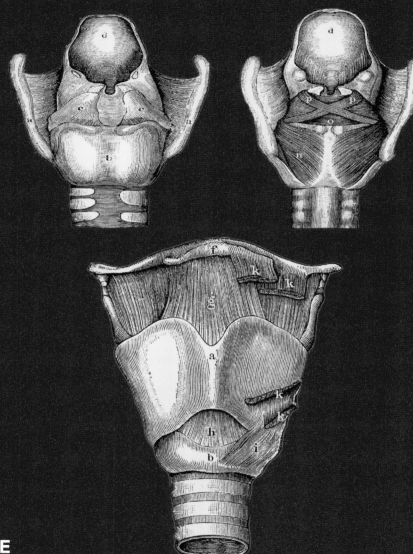

THE

LARYNX

DETAIL

The Larynx Front

trigger a little upward and forward movement beneath your fingers. You might come to appreciate from this experiment that in order to access your full range of notes, your larynx has to be able to move freely. Tension in the jaw or tongue will impede its movement and you may find higher notes difficult to sing.

The vocal folds

Your vocal folds, or vocal cords, have three functions: opening, which allows you to breathe; closing, which protects your windpipe; and vibrating together, which initiates sound. The two vocal folds sit front to back across your larynx and vibrate against each other when the air from your lungs passes through them. Men's vocal folds are longer and thicker than women's, measuring 1.75cm–2.5cm, while female vocal folds are between 1.25cm–1.75cm.

Here's the geeky bit that is worth knowing; the combination of the shape of your vocal folds and the speed of their vibration dictates which note is produced.

However, you have no conscious control over vocal-fold shape or the speed of vibration. A combination of good posture, core muscle engagement (which I cover in the Breathing for singing chapter) and a vocal tract without unwanted tension (page 66), will enable any change in shape or speed to happen naturally. These disciplines can be learned, and I will go through each of them for you in this book.

Vocal-fold vibration – not absolutely vital to know to sing well, but pretty interesting!

Different speeds of vibration will produce different pitches of notes. The faster the vibration, the higher the frequency; the slower the vibration, the lower the frequency. This principle applies to all sound, not just the voice. If you clap your hands slowly and then gradually get really fast, you should hear the sound getting higher as the vibrations in the air speed up.

Vocal-fold shape

The vocal folds are attached to the inside of the main cartilages that form the protective tube of the larynx (the bit that moves when you swallow). It is the movement of these cartilages that causes the vocal folds to change shape.

Your vocal folds are constantly changing shape and texture in a variety of combinations between short and thick to long and thin. High notes are produced by the vocal folds stretching and thinning and low notes are formed by shorter and fatter vocal-fold shaping.

Try 'twanging' a rubber band hooked between your thumbs; you will see that as you stretch the band the twanging sound becomes more high pitched, and as you release the tension the band becomes shorter and thicker and the sound becomes deeper. The same principle applies to guitar strings: the thinner ones produce the higher sounds and the fatter ones create a more bass-heavy sound.

A look inside your mouth

You will need a mirror for this.

The epiglottis

If you look inside your mouth with a mirror, you will see a flap of tissue at the back of your throat just at the top of your larynx; this is the epiglottis, and its job is to close over the larynx to prevent food and foreign bodies from passing into your airways when you swallow.

Touching the epiglottis will trigger your gag reflex.

The pharynx

The pharynx is the area at the back of your throat. Take a look and you will see two arches on either side of your throat, with the tonsils (unless they have been surgically removed) just peeking out and the epiglottis positioned in between. The dangly bit suspended from above is called the uvula and is not directly involved in singing.

Try moaning UH, as though you are a whingeing child complaining about being told to go to bed, and you should feel a gentle squeeze and narrowing of the back of your throat. This should feel effortless, so don't push. This is a really useful vocal-tract shape in singing; it can help you increase volume and produce a twangy quality of sound, popular in contemporary singing. Now alternate the whingeing child with a big, open-throated, slightly breathy 'UH' and feel the difference in the shape at the back of your throat. After a few tries you should be able to feel a smaller space at the back of your throat with the moaning and then a bigger space with the sighing. Be patient with yourself as it might take a while to get this, but it's worth the effort. Next, see if you can sing a phrase from a song with the twangy, moaning quality and then sing the same phrase with a more open-throated, breathy quality. You are doing this for self-awareness and to develop different qualities of sound that are useful in conveying emotion. Additionally, the moaning shape is also strategically helpful when it comes to singing higher notes.

The soft palate – eliminating nasality

If you use your tongue to trace the roof of your mouth from your front teeth to the back of your mouth you will feel a sudden change in texture from bony to soft tissue. This soft tissue is your soft palate, a

THE MOUTH

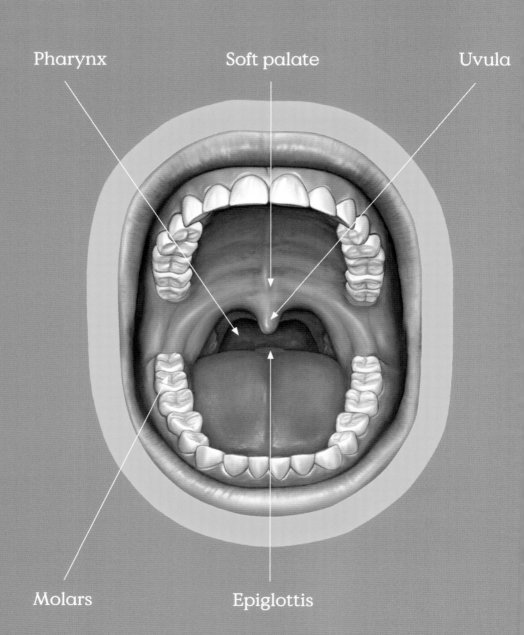

Pharynx

Soft palate

Uvula

Molars

Epiglottis

moveable structure that directs airflow either to your nose or mouth, or both at the same time, according to how it is positioned. This structure is commonly described as 'the door to the nose'. The onset of a yawn (the first second of movement), will give you the sense of lifting the soft palate and therefore closing the door to the nose. Do be aware that taking a yawn a bit further will push the back of your tongue downwards, which is not desirable. Alternatively, imagining sniffing something nice, 'smiling on the inside' or sucking on a ice-lolly can all encourage the lifting of the soft palate.

Sounding nasal

Note that a little bit of sound down the nose, described as 'nasalised singing', can be appropriate for some types of commercial music. It is not the same thing as sounding nasal, which is generally considered undesirable.

If your singing persistently sounds nasal, your soft palate might be positioned in such a way that it is allowing your air (therefore your sound) to flow out through your nose. To test for nasality in your singing, try singing a sustained AH sound and then, after a few seconds, pinch your nostrils closed for one second while still singing. Do this a few times. If you hear no difference in sound when you pinch your nose, then this would indicate that all of the air is being directed through your mouth and that you are singing with an appropriately positioned soft palate. If the sound changes when you pinch your nose, you will know that there must be air coming through your nose; if so, try to adjust the position of your soft palate by recreating that sense of sniffing something pleasant or the onset of a yawn. Keep doing this and keep testing until there is no change in sound when you pinch your nose. Please be patient; this can take practice.

Learn to feel the difference between opening and closing your soft palate by singing NG-GAH. NG directs all of the air to your nose, so if

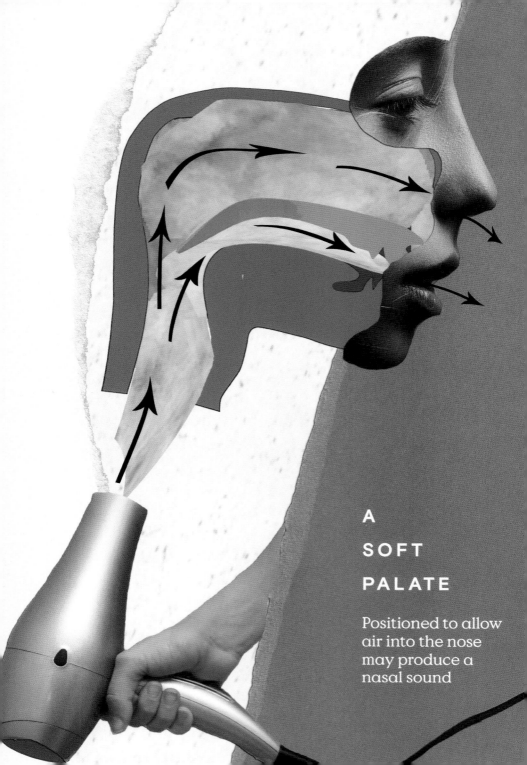

A

SOFT

PALATE

Positioned to allow
air into the nose
may produce a
nasal sound

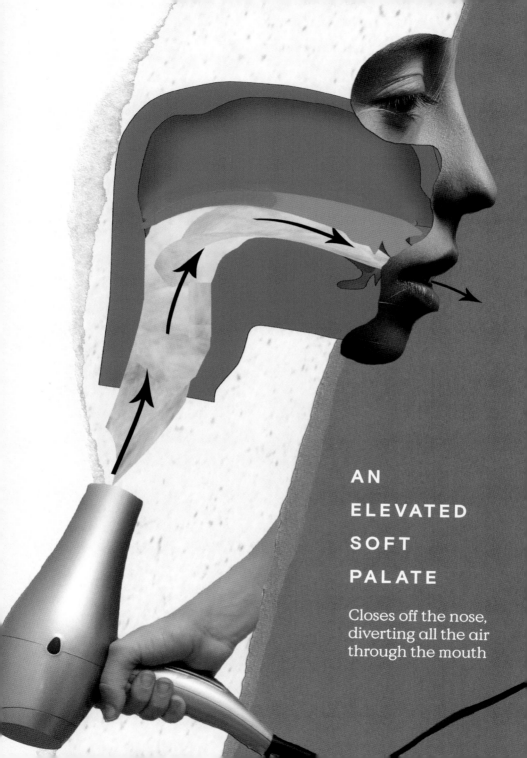

AN ELEVATED SOFT PALATE

Closes off the nose, diverting all the air through the mouth you pinch your nostrils on NG, the sound should stop altogether, while the vowel in GAH allows you to create a big space that includes lifting the soft palate. This should give you the extremes of each position: closed and open.

The tongue

Your tongue is huge. Only thirty percent of it is visible inside your mouth; the rest of its mass is in your throat and under your chin. Its sheer size can make it an asset or a liability in singing. Your tongue plays a major role in shaping the airspaces in your vocal tract and is also vital in forming words. Positioning it incorrectly can interfere with airflow and therefore reduce resonance, and tongue tension can put unwelcome pressure on the larynx, preventing it from moving freely.

What is the best position for the tongue in singing?

The tongue's general resting position is lying relaxed on the floor of the mouth with the tip resting against the back of the bottom front teeth. If you say the ABC you will feel that the tip is mostly touching the bottom teeth. During singing the tip remains mostly in this position but there is also a gentle sense of the very back of the tongue standing a little bit high and forward and away from the back of the throat. A tongue that is drawn backward, towards the throat, will impede your airflow and may muffle or dampen your sound.

Keeping the tip of your tongue behind your bottom front teeth, open your mouth and try and stretch your tongue out of your throat. Hold it for about five seconds and repeat. You should get a sense of space behind the back of the tongue. Try this a few times and make yourself familiar with this sensation. If you are not used to stretching the tongue, it might be a little bit uncomfortable at first, so to start with stretch it only as far as it wants to go. A good way to exercise it and improve its

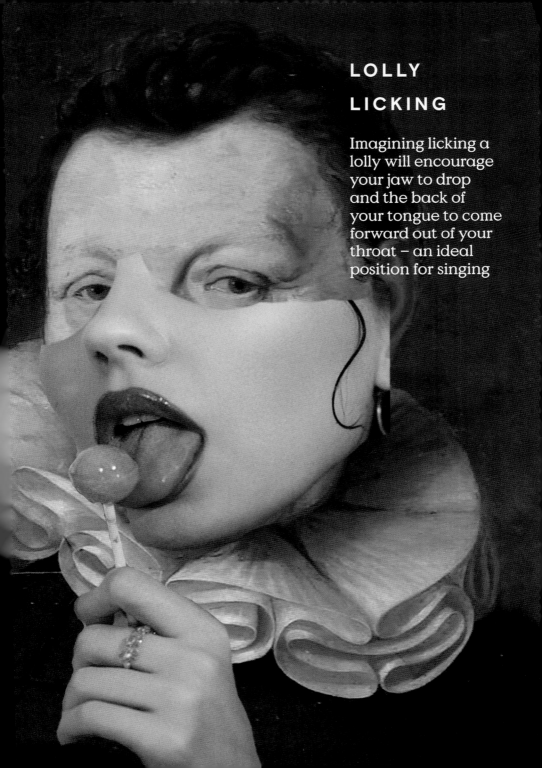

LOLLY

LICKING

Imagining licking a lolly will encourage your jaw to drop and the back of your tongue to come forward out of your throat – an ideal position for singing

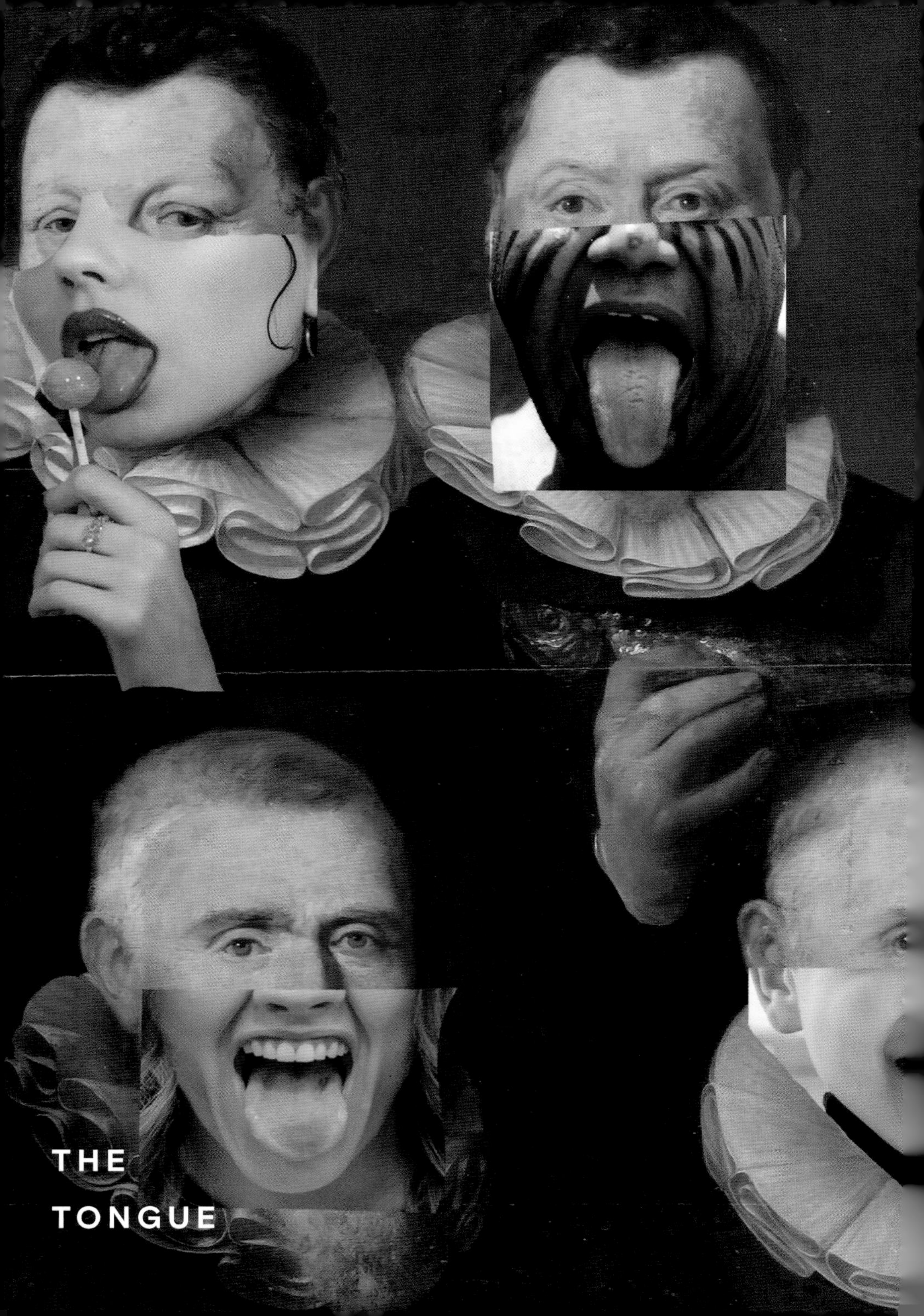
THE
TONGUE

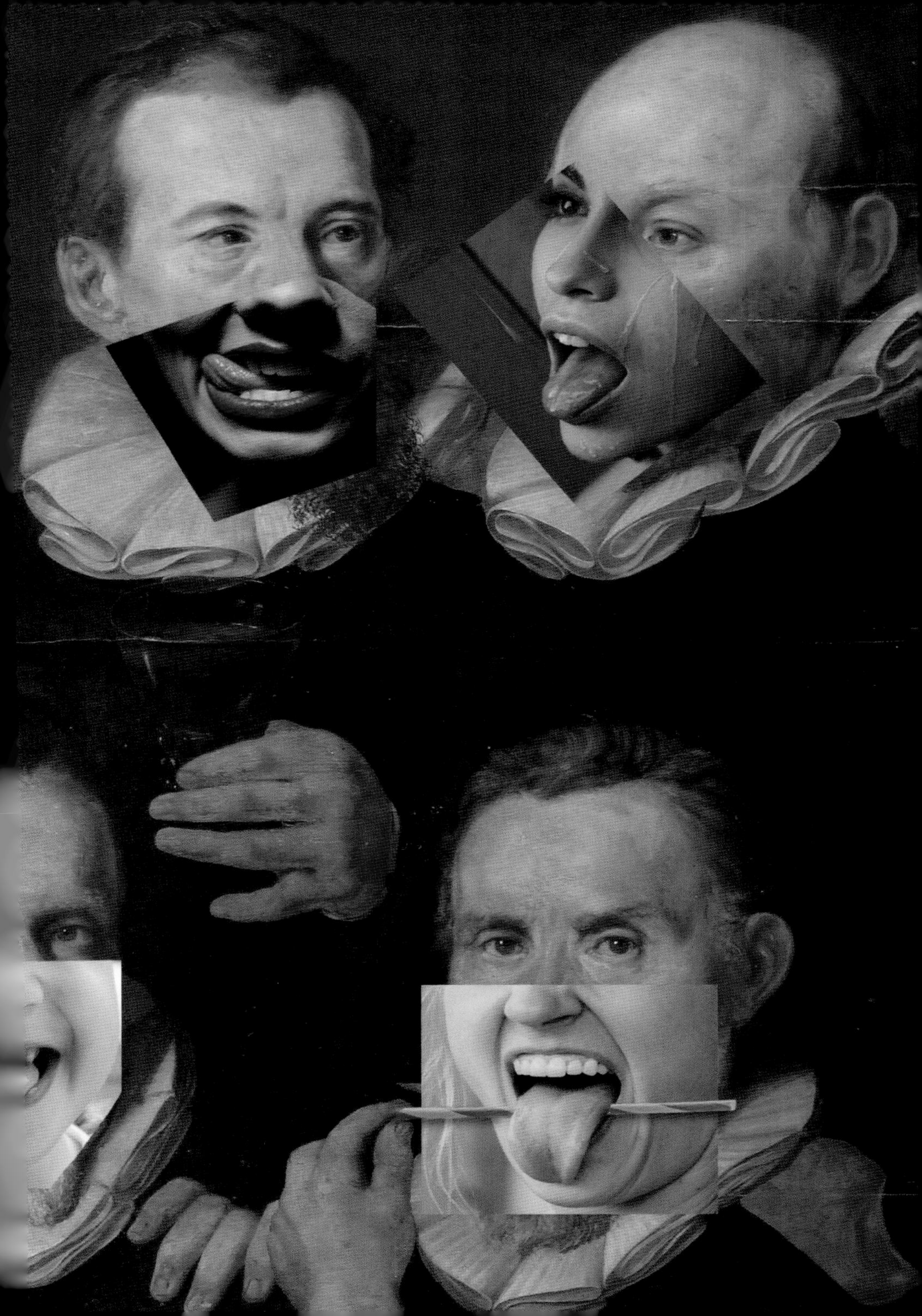

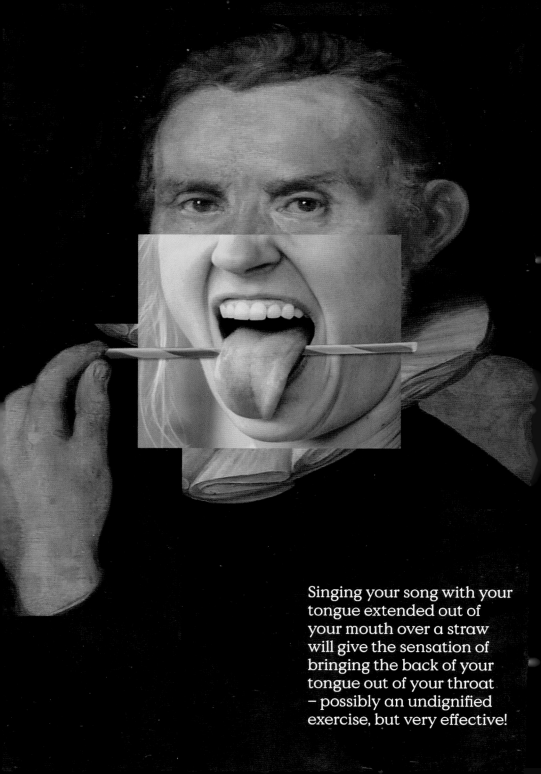

Singing your song with your tongue extended out of your mouth over a straw will give the sensation of bringing the back of your tongue out of your throat – possibly an undignified exercise, but very effective!

tone is to draw circles inside your cheeks or to clean your teeth with it. As we get older, we lose tone in our tongues, which can make talking hard work, so it's worth giving it a regular workout.

Now you have experienced the sensation of drawing your tongue out of your throat, here's an exercise to achieve this 'forward tongue' sensation while singing. Relax your jaw open and place a straw (or pencil, or chopstick) across your bottom front teeth. You need to hold on to the straw with your hand to avoid gripping it with your tongue. Stretch your tongue out over the top of it, so the tip is hanging out of your mouth. Your focus is on getting your tongue away from your throat rather than stretching it out of your mouth.

Looking in the mirror, sing 'Happy Birthday' without allowing your tongue to go back into your mouth behind the straw. Don't worry about not being able to form the words properly, the point is to keep the back of your tongue in a forward position away from the back of your throat. You may find that OH and UU are quite challenging and notice that your tongue will instinctively want to draw back into your throat. Don't let it. Once you've done this a few times, remove the straw and place the tip of your tongue behind your bottom front teeth and continue to sing with that new sense of the tongue being forward away from the back of your throat. If it feels uncomfortable, try dropping the jaw open a little bit more. This is an outstanding exercise that can improve overall sound quality and make singing feel easier.

Vowel shaping

The tongue is extremely important in shaping vowels. The written vowels of A, E, I, O and U are often sung differently to the way that you might read them on a page or say them out loud. This is because the spoken vowels require the tongue to reposition itself in ways that can close down the resonating spaces, which will feel, and sound, uncomfortable when singing. Learning how to form vowels without impeding the airflow through the resonating spaces is therefore very useful.

There are no hard and fast rules about vowel shaping because there are so many factors at play, including your accent, the language of the song, the style of the music and your personal tastes. For example, it is normal in classical music for a lyric soprano who is singing at the top of her range to reshape her vowels; if sustaining UU (like the word 'you') at a certain pitch is going to be troublesome, she will 'reshape' it to sound more like an AW (so it will sound something like 'yore'), which will feel easier for her to produce with resonance. This can occasionally lead to compromises in the clarity of her diction but the quality of the sound will be maintained through the phrase, which is a feature of that style of music. Similarly, the 'y' sound at the end of the word 'boy' (this sound is called a diphthong) can be difficult to sing in certain contexts, so singers often drop it in favour of letting the predominant vowel sound linger (OH) or by leaving the diphthong until the last millisecond and making it barely audible. There will also be occasions when singers make a stylistic choice to sing through the diphthong, sustaining the EE sound at the end of the word instead: Boh-EE.

There are lots of options available to you, but I don't want you to feel overloaded, so you should do what feels physically comfortable and stylistically appropriate. When certain words feel difficult, experiment with your tongue shape to change the sound of the vowel and see if that helps. Bear in mind that a word that is easy to sing in your lower range is not necessarily going to be easy to produce in your higher range.

Diphthongs

A **diphthong** is a sound that is perceived as a single vowel sound but actually combines two vowels in one syllable. For example, as outlined

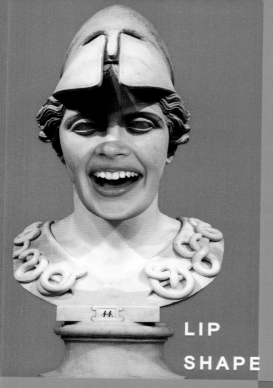

LIP

SHAPE

CHANGES

EVERYTHING

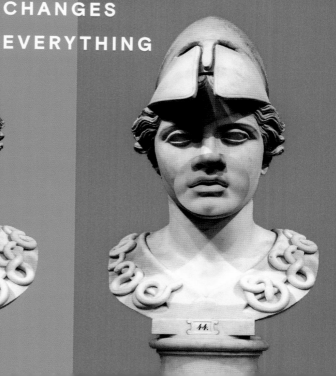

VOWEL SHAPING

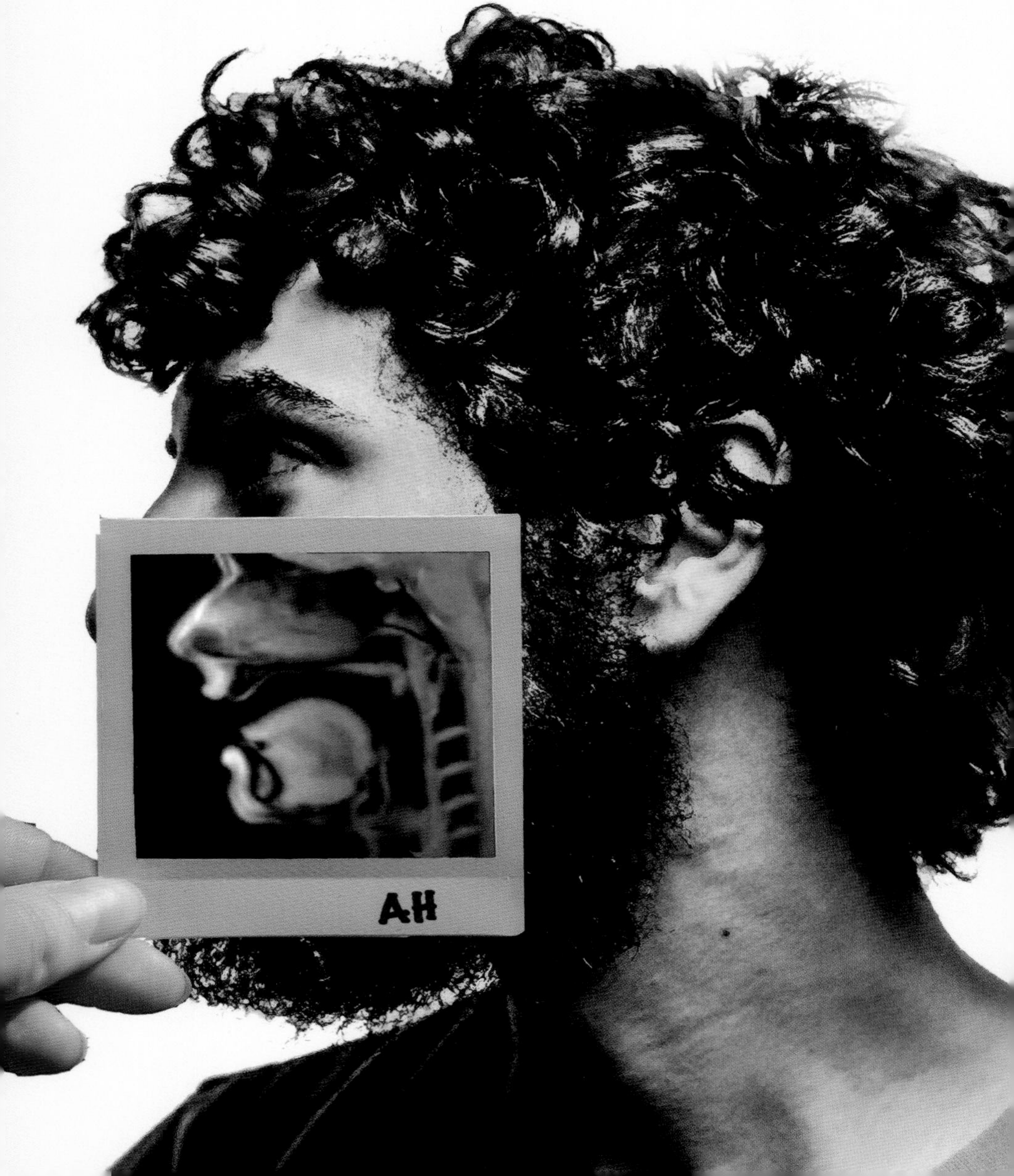
AH

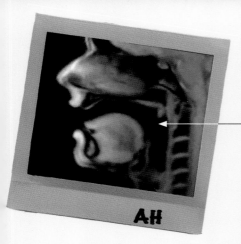

AH

The black space is the airspace. Letting your tongue go back towards your throat may impede the free flow of air. Be aware

Note the shape and size of the tongue as it changes vowels

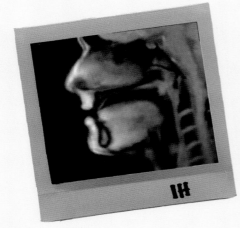

IH

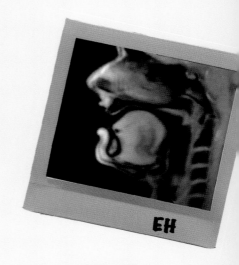

EH

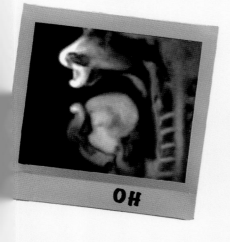

OH

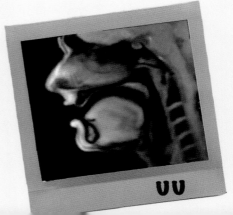

UU

THE LIPS

Experiment with drawing your lips back and protruding the top front teeth and see how the sound changes

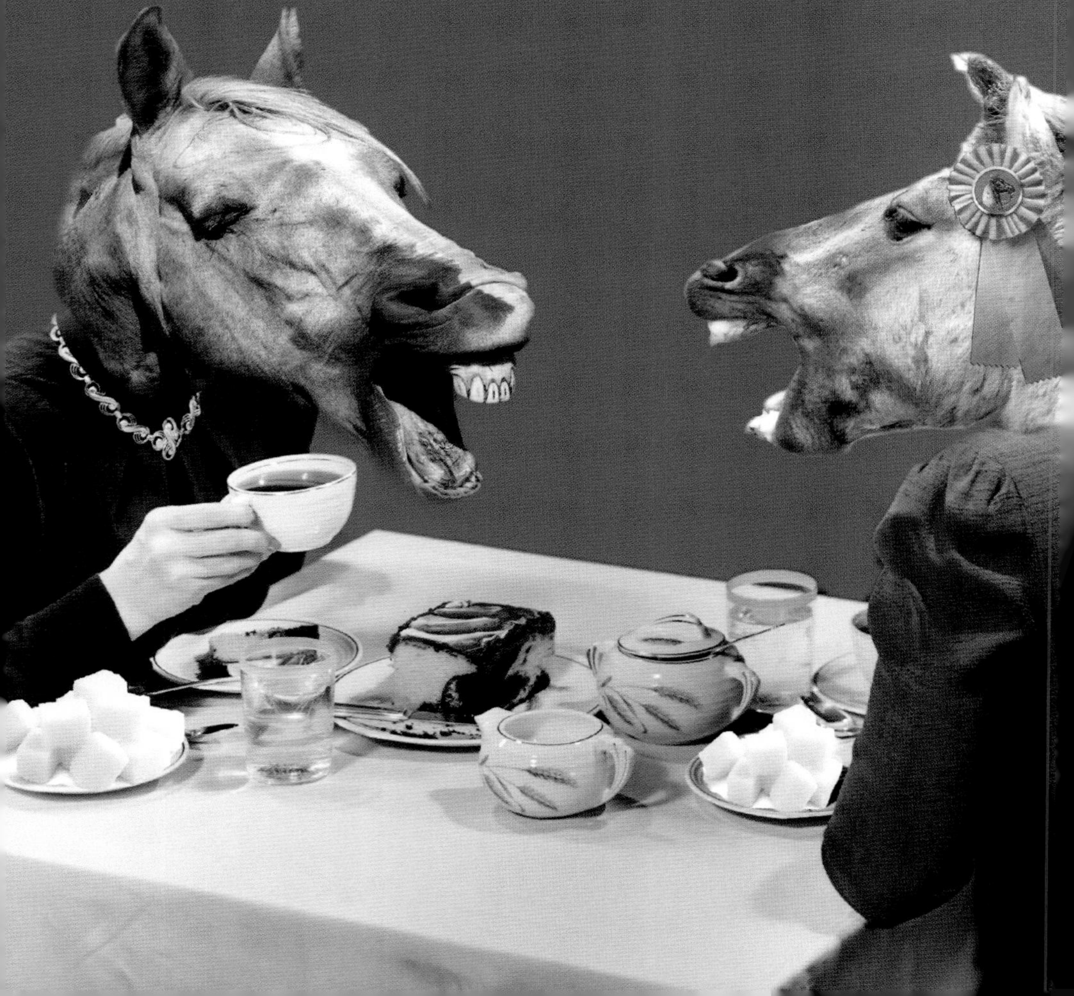

above, the word 'boy' has an OH sound allowed by EE. The sound begins in one vowel sound and morphs towards another.

Say A, E, I, O, U slowly out loud a few times and notice the movements of the tongue and the width of your jaw space. Your tongue will feel generally quite flat and each of the vowels require two movements: A(y), E(eh), I(y), O(h), (y)U. Now open your jaw a little and try this 'singers' version: EH (air), IH (it), AH (dark), OH (Australia) UU (glue). You should notice that these vowels have smoother transitions between them as there is less movement of the tongue and the sound will be a little louder, too. You should be able to keep the back of your tongue away from the throat while still allowing for the tip to rest comfortably behind the bottom front teeth. In singing, the rear section of your tongue should be positioned away from your throat, irrespective of the vowels you are forming.

The lips

The position and shape of your lips hugely impacts any sound you make. Drawing your lips back into a smiling position will brighten the sound, while pouting them forward into a 'trout pout' will produce a darker tone. Then there are all the positions between those extremes to experiment with. Watch and copy your favourite singers performing live and see what kinds of shapes they are using and how those shapes might impact your own sound.

The jaw

Many of us hold tension in our jaw, which is guaranteed to have an adverse effect on the sound we make when we sing. The good news is that with self-awareness and a few simple exercises we can learn to relax our jaw and really improve our singing.

If you feel tension in your jaw generally, not just in singing, try massaging the large muscles in your cheeks; sit down on a chair with your elbows leaning on your thighs and allow your face to drop down on to your fists, using them to massage your cheeks with circular movements. This can be quite painful, but will loosen up any tightness in this area, and the resulting relaxation feels great.

When it comes to singing, you should always maintain a sense of space between your upper and lower back teeth. Practise singing with one finger placed sideways between your back teeth – in a comfortable position, not too far back. Your teeth should just rest on your finger and not clamp down on it; biting down on your finger will be an indicator that you are tending to clench, and it will hurt! You won't be able to articulate words very well in this position, but don't worry about that for now.

Once you feel that your jaw is a comfortable width apart for singing, remove your finger and carry on singing, maintaining that same sense of distance between your upper and lower molars. Check yourself in the mirror and make sure that the degree of opening remains at the minimum finger-width distance and doesn't start to close.

> Opening your mouth too widely will reduce the size of the resonating space at the back of your throat

If you experiment further, you may find that some vowels are easier to sing if you hold your jaw in a slightly wider position.

When you are singing and speaking your jaw should move straight up and down. Make sure that you are not moving it sideways or that you are not over-opening to the point that you can feel a popping sensation

KEEPING SPACE BETWEEN THE MOLARS

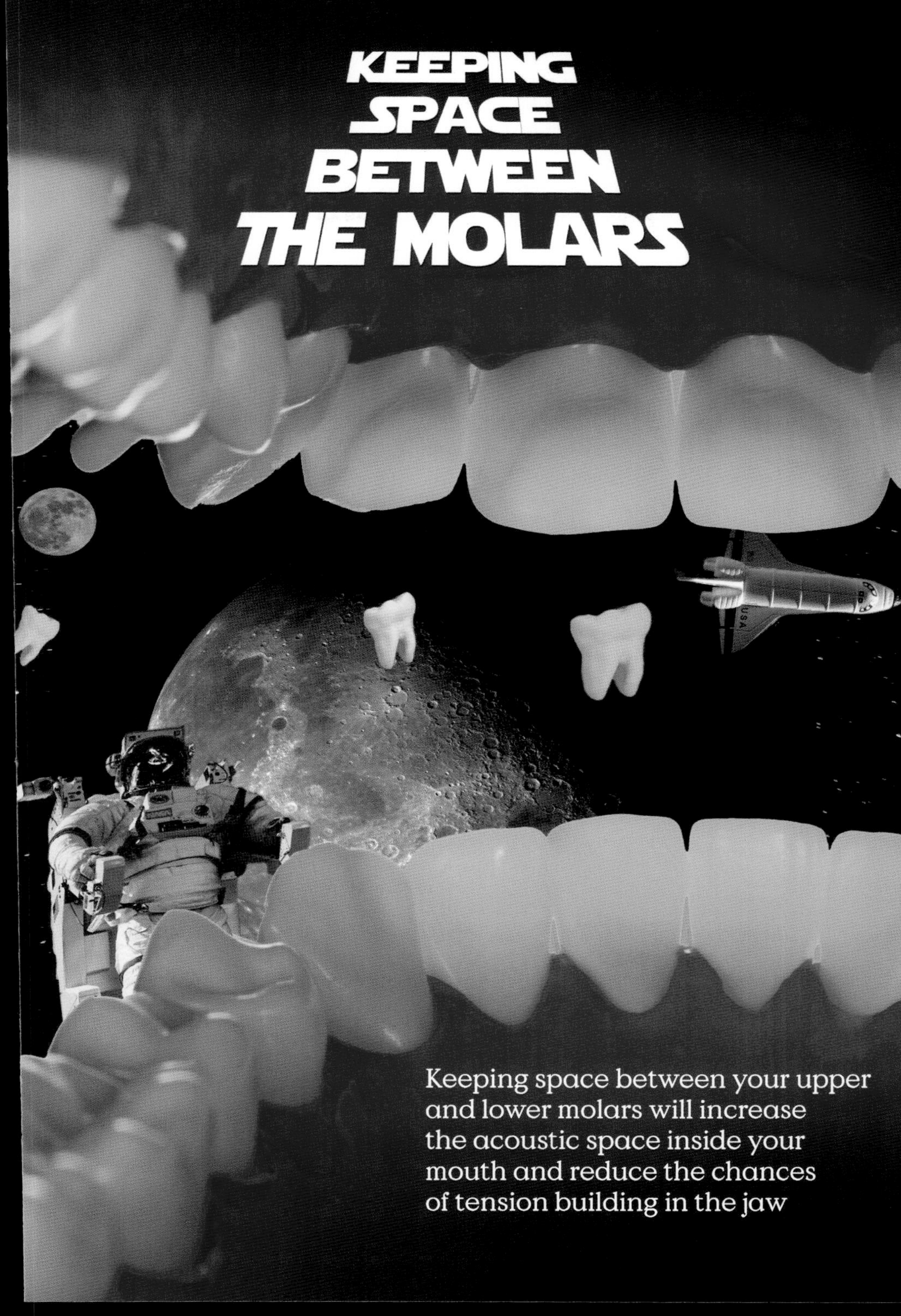

Keeping space between your upper and lower molars will increase the acoustic space inside your mouth and reduce the chances of tension building in the jaw

THE FACE

Imagining sniffing a flower will brighten the sound

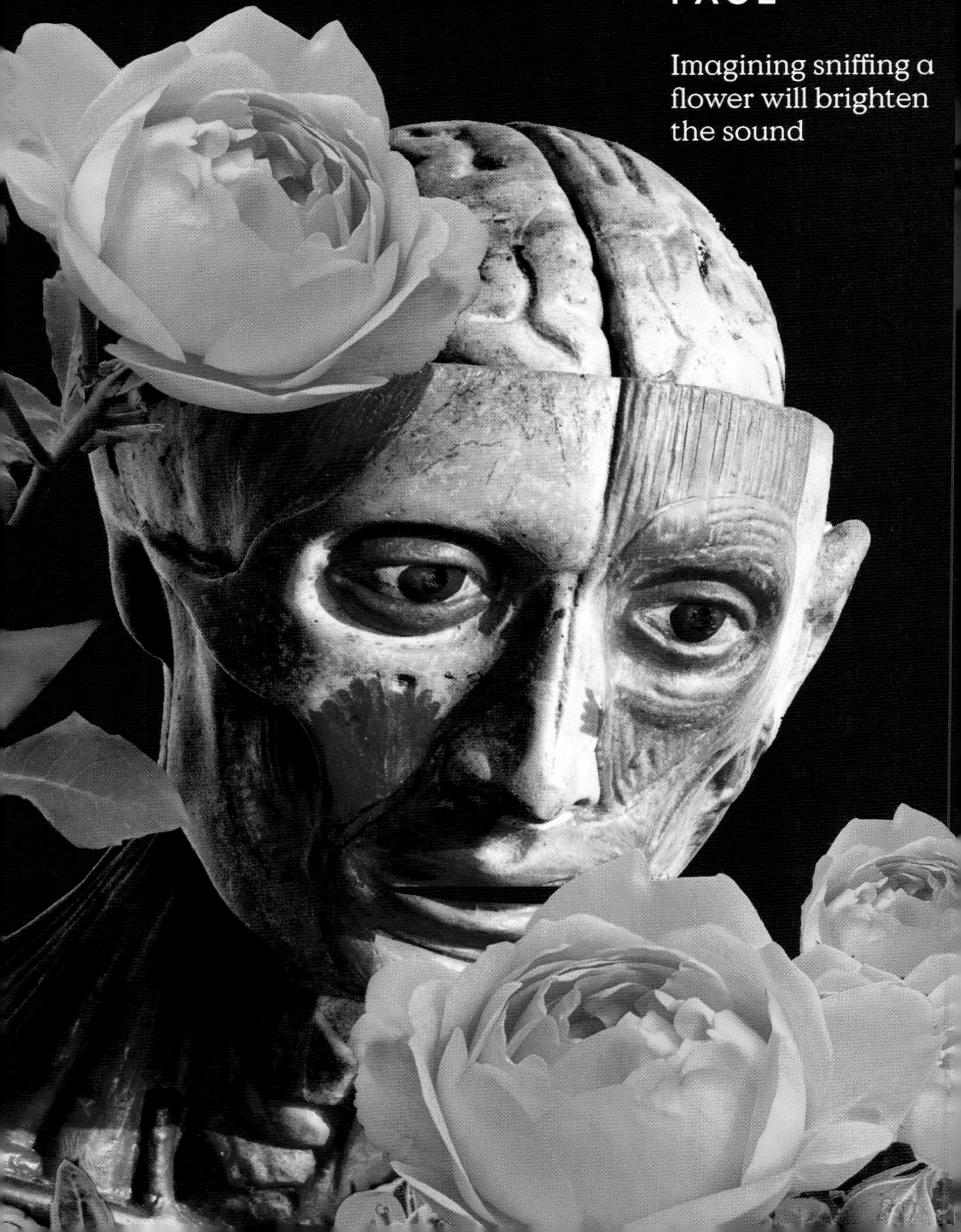

in the joint. A very wide jaw will reduce the space at the back of your throat and diminish your chances of producing a deliciously resonant sound. It will also be tiring and may lead to tension.

If you observe that there is a lot of extreme movement in your jaw while you sing, take some time to work on making smaller and smoother movements.

The face

Imagine that you are sniffing an incredibly beautifully fragranced flower – feel your forehead and eyebrows lifting, your nostrils flaring and see if you can also feel the back of the roof of your mouth tightening. This change in your mouth's resonating space will give a 'brightening' effect. It can work like magic while you sing. Get sniffing!

If it feels easy, it will sound good

Resonating spaces

Now you've had an introduction to the integral parts of your vocal tract you should be starting to appreciate how the manipulation of any of them will alter the shape of the airspace and that any change in these resonating spaces, no matter how small, will impact the sound in both good and bad ways. The best way to learn is to experiment with your instrument. If something feels or sounds uncomfortable, try to work out what you might adjust to make it feel easier. If it feels easy, it will sound good.

CHAPTER

FIVE

TENSION

IS

YOUR

ENEMY

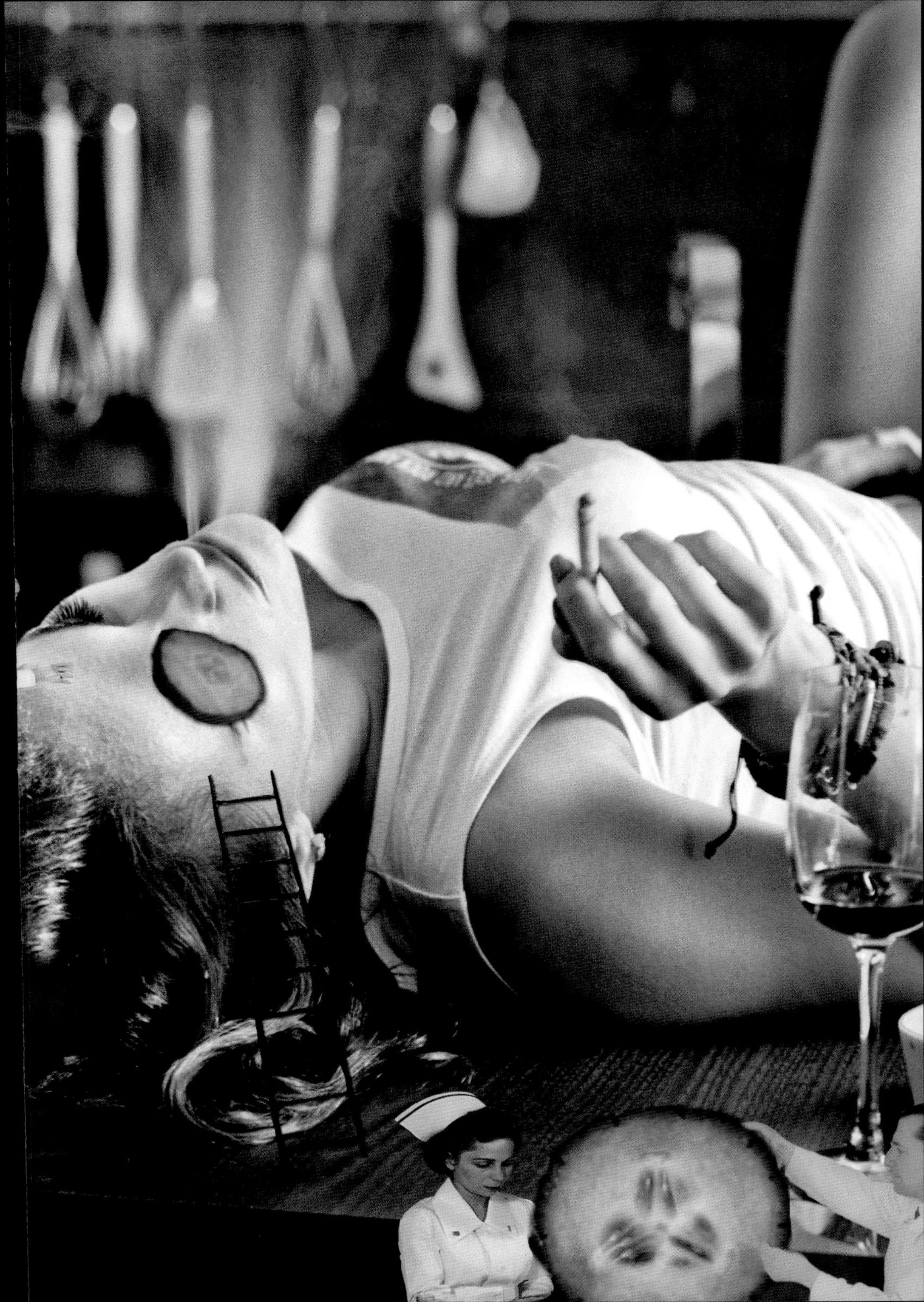

Tension is your enemy

Tension in any part
of the vocal tract will
make your singing sound
and feel effortful

If your singing feels or sounds uncomfortable you may have inadvertently introduced unwanted tension into your vocal tract. This tension can be generated by a number of factors, both external to and intrinsic to singing; a bad day at the office, road rage or general anxiety but the most common culprit is the use of excessive effort.

A methodical warm-up, like the one I suggest later (page 108), will ease tension and oxygenate the muscles and get them working efficiently. Stiff, cold or stressed muscles will not be responsive and are more likely to strain. You will know if you are not warm, as your singing will not feel comfortable.

If, while you are singing, you find you are straining to hit certain notes or you can't seem to get the sensation of resonance, try one of the following relaxation methods.

- **Laugh** – pure and simple! Laughing reduces stress in the vocal tract immediately. It is the single most effective method of stress release there is. I regularly get students to laugh their way through songs, particularly on the trickier passages. The pure silliness is enough to make some singers stop worrying.

- **The silent laugh** Close your eyes and say 'huh' a few times very, very quietly. Almost inaudibly. Now say 'huh' again but completely silently. You should experience a release of tension in the throat. It feels nice. It's worth spending a bit of time on this. This is referred to by the singing community as 'silent laughter' and is often described as 'smiling across the throat'.

> Laughing reduces stress in the vocal tract immediately

- **Jaw and lips** Drop your jaw so your upper and lower molars are about a finger-width apart (roughly 0.5–1cm). Relax your tongue with the tip snuggled behind the bottom front teeth. Now close your lips gently and start to hum until there is vibration in your lips. Keep humming on any note and then, without losing this vibration or space between the molars, hum on a note that is in the range of the song you are singing. When you feel relaxed, go from humming into singing while maintaining that same sense of ease.

CHAPTER

SIX

POSTURE

FOR

SINGING

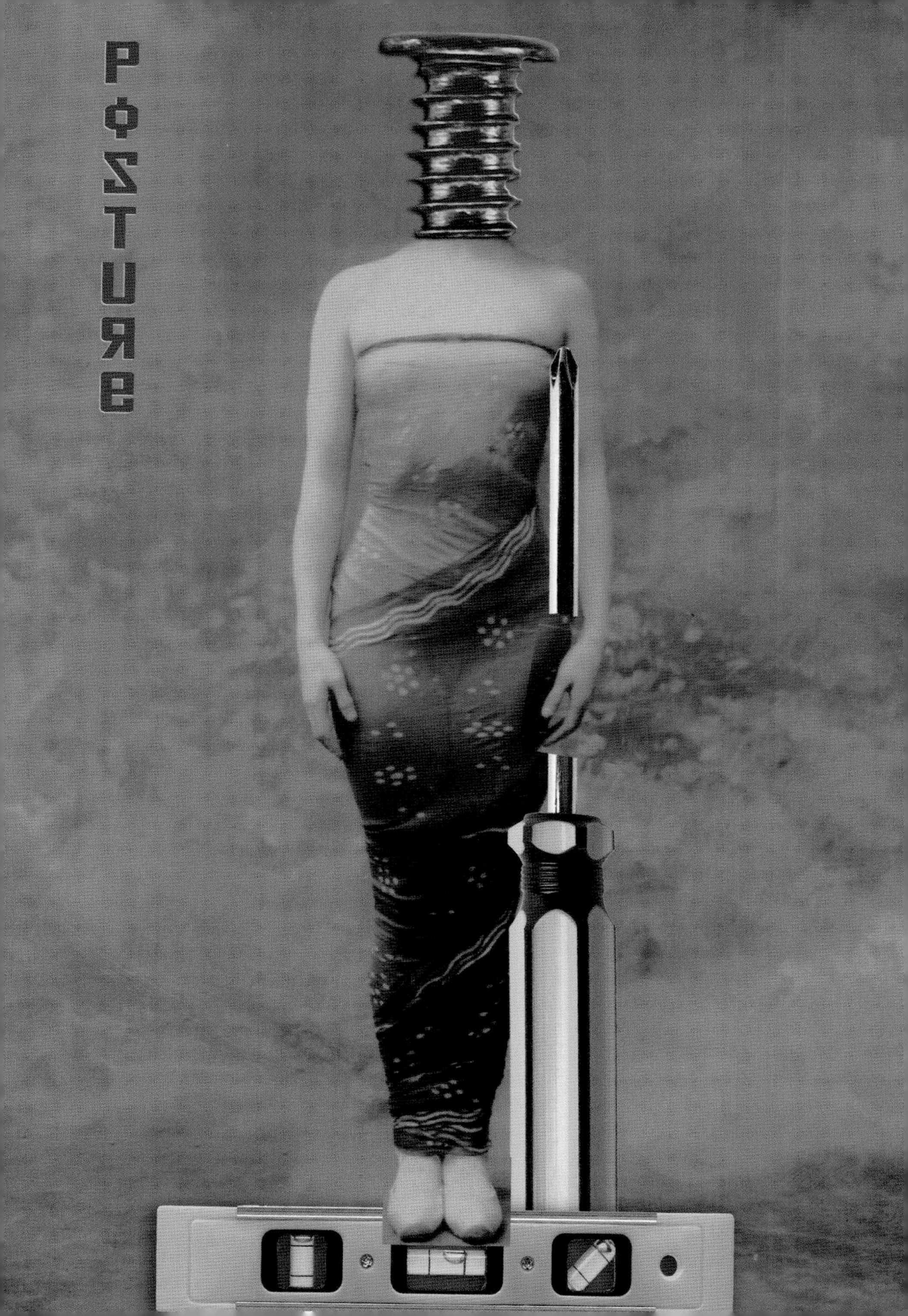
POSTURE

Posture for singing

It is not the keys on the piano nor the throat in the singer that creates sound, but the whole body working as an instrument

You can't sing well with poor physical alignment. It really is that simple.

It is not the keys on the piano nor the throat in the singer that creates sound, but the whole body working as an instrument. Good posture and its positive effect on breathing makes an enormous difference, not only to the quality of the sound you make in singing but also to your wider good health.

Imagine a guitar made of rubber, rather than wood. No matter how much precision you apply to your fingering, the instability of the instrument's body simply won't allow for the strings to achieve the required level of tension to play in tune. A warped soundboard in the finest looking piano, played by an expert, will sound out of tune. Slumped shoulders and a collapsed chest in a singer will restrict the amount of air they can take in and will impact the tuning and quality of the sound they make. Posture is everything.

What is good posture for singing?

Good posture, in general terms, gives a sense of the whole body standing tall, or lengthening vertically, while being firmly grounded. You should feel strong and balanced, with a sense of purpose and never tense or stiff.

Posture checklist

Some singers find it useful to 'checklist' the body in sections and imagine stacking them in vertical alignment: head, neck, shoulders, chest, pelvis, knees and feet. Imagining a small cushion of air between each vertebrae of the spine can also be helpful in achieving good posture.

Feel the base of your skull with your fingers (this is the occipital bone) and you will become aware of the area of soft tissue immediately below it. There are lots of muscles connected here, including some that are connected to your eyeballs (look right and left and you will feel them) and some that connect to the hyoid bone from which your voice box is suspended. In the Shaping the sound chapter, you will have learned that effective vocal production relies on the free movement of the voice box; good posture includes keeping your head in alignment with your neck to allow for this. There are also muscles under your chin that attach to the hyoid bone, so pushing your chin up, out or in can have outcomes for your voice box.

I like to include the jaw in postural set-up. Tightness in the jaw can manifest itself in the near closing of your back molars, which impacts the size and shape of the acoustic space at the back of the throat. You should always feel as if you have space between your upper and lower molars when you sing. This can be extremely useful for people who clench or grind their teeth.

THE DROPPED STERNUM

Take care! A dropped sternum will cause your shoulders to slump and ribcage to collapse

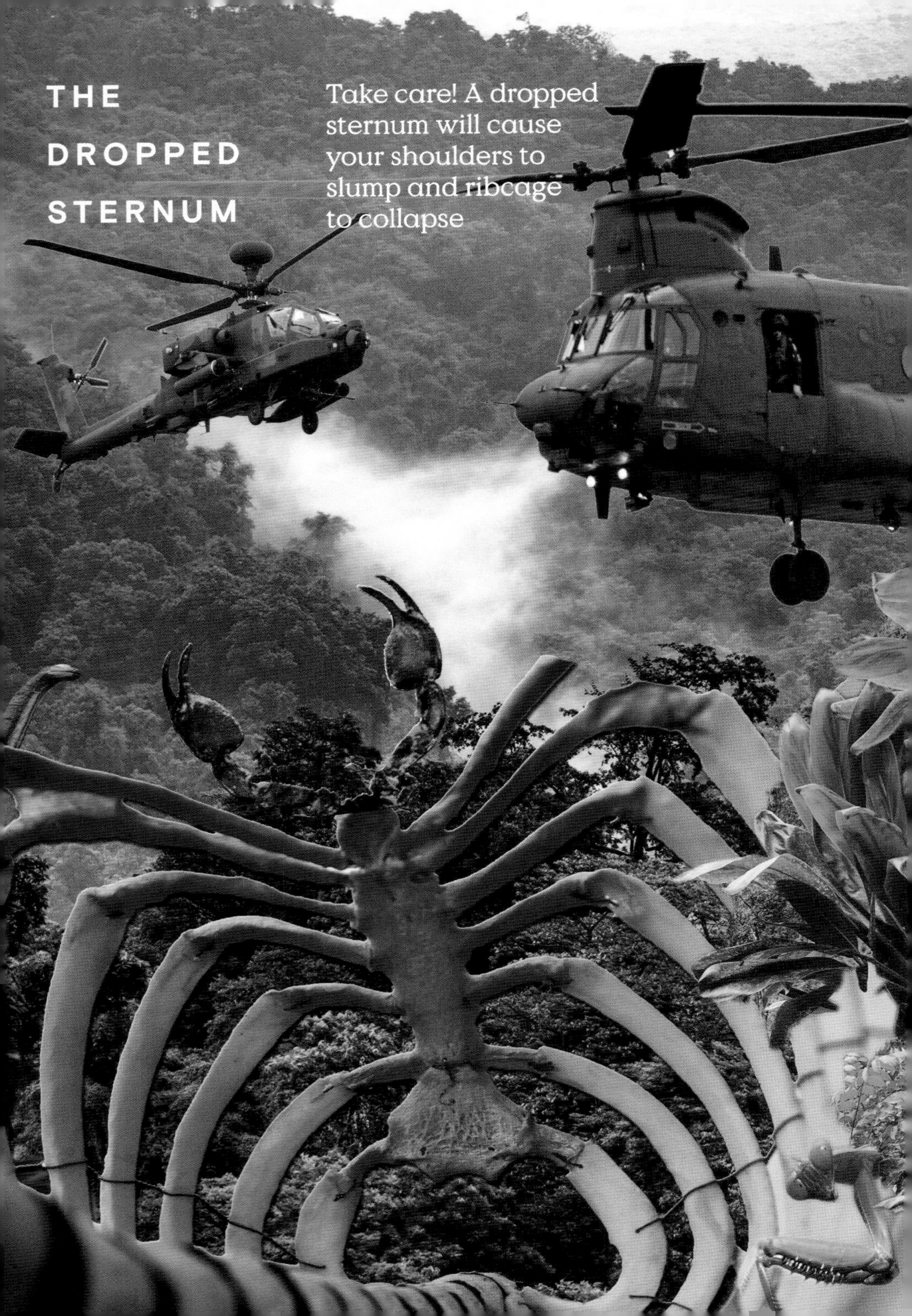

If you wear bifocal or half-moon glasses, be aware that tilting your head to see over or through your lenses can negatively impact your head/neck alignment. I can't offer a solution to this, I'm afraid, but I do want to flag it up.

The sternum is the bone that runs down the centre of your chest and to which your ribs are attached. Place a finger at the base of the sternum and lift it by about 1.5cm. You should feel it tip forward and up. Holding this lifted sternum posture, you will immediately experience the sensation of an open chest, with your shoulders slotting comfortably back and down. Note that this is a gentle repositioning of your sternum, and not the upheaval of your entire ribcage towards your shoulders, which generates stress around the neck. Now try dropping your sternum by about 1.5cm to feel the difference (watch your finger) – you will feel your shoulders and ribcage collapse. This really is a tip worth trying.

Arching your back or sticking your bum out while singing can inhibit your breathing, so try tucking your pelvis or tail bone under without losing your overall body height. I have heard tales of strict singing teachers making their students stand on piles of books with their heels hanging over the edge to encourage the repositioning of the pelvis. Standing on the edge of a step does the same thing and is probably more dignified. My students experience a noticeable improvement in breathing efficiency when they consciously 'tuck under'.

Postural set-up

You will need a mirror for this postural set-up.

- Stand with your feet flat on the floor, hip-width apart.

- Imagine a thread from your crown to the ceiling. Let it lift the

POSTURAL SET UP

Jaw relaxed, neck long, shoulders back, tail bone tucked under

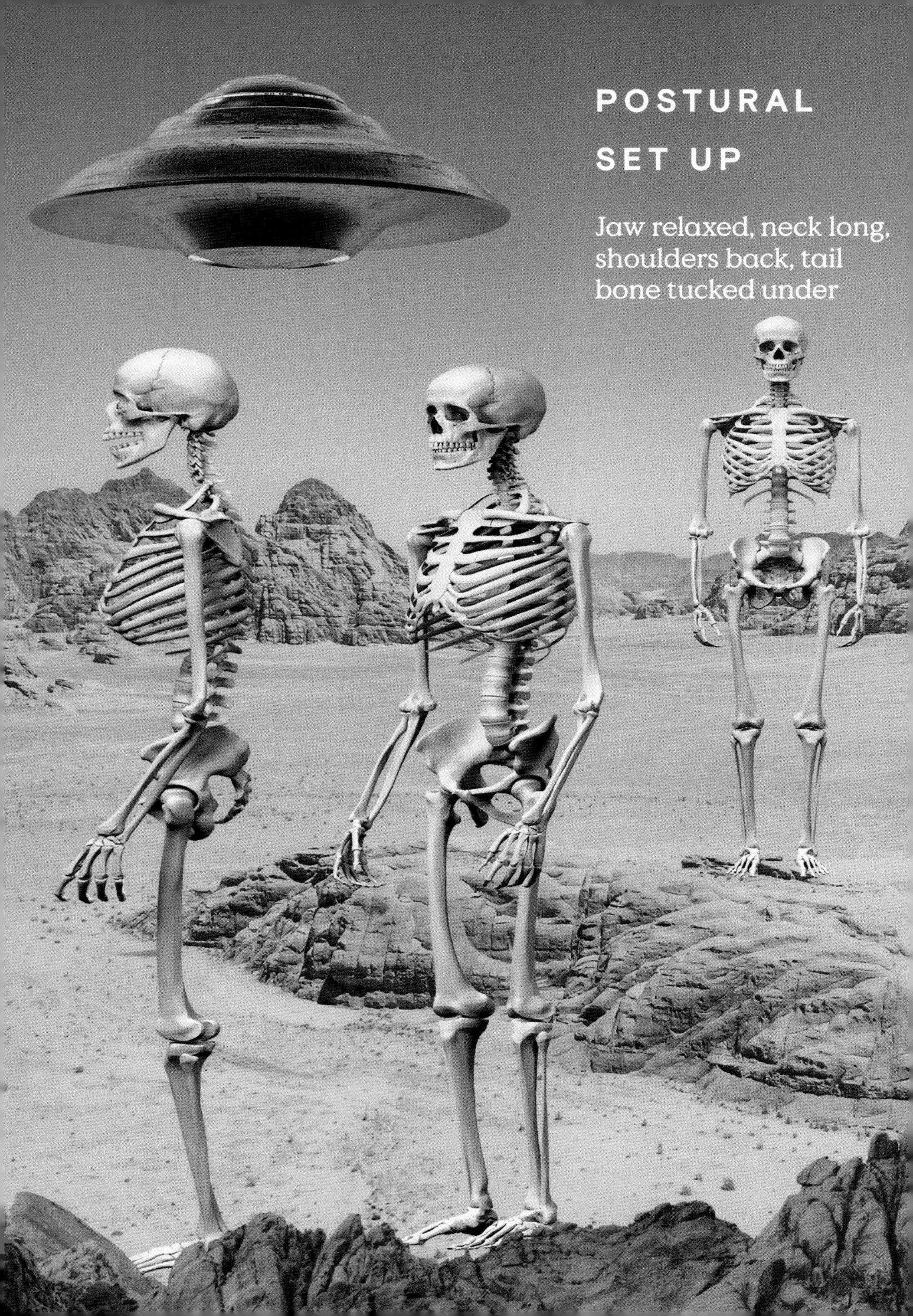

CHAPTER SIX – POSTURE FOR SINGING

weight of your head off your neck and allow the back of your neck to lengthen.

- Drop your jaw open a little to a relaxed position, keeping a finger-width gap (roughly 0.5–1cm) between your upper and lower molars. Keep a neutral chin position.

- Open your shoulders by gently turning the tops of your arms out in their sockets so the palms of your hands are facing just slightly forward. Your shoulders should be back and down and shoulder blades drawn down towards your waist, without strain.

- Place a finger on your sternum and tilt the sternum forward and upward by about 1.5cm. You may get a sense of your chest facing the ceiling.

- Turn sideways-on to the mirror and, without losing overall height, manipulate your pelvis or tail bone so it is tucked underneath you.

- Knees should be soft as opposed to 'locked'.

- Your feet need to be firmly planted, but not leaden or cemented. A wonderful singing teacher friend, Anne Leatherland, describes this feeling as the 'goalie's stance'. Firm, yet ready to move in any direction at a moment's notice. Perfect.

You should have an overall sense of height and physical self-confidence, without strain or stress anywhere in the body.

You're ready to go!

MAINTAIN

LENGTH

Down the back of
the neck and space
between the chest
and under the chin

CHAPTER

SEVEN

BREATHING

FOR

SINGING

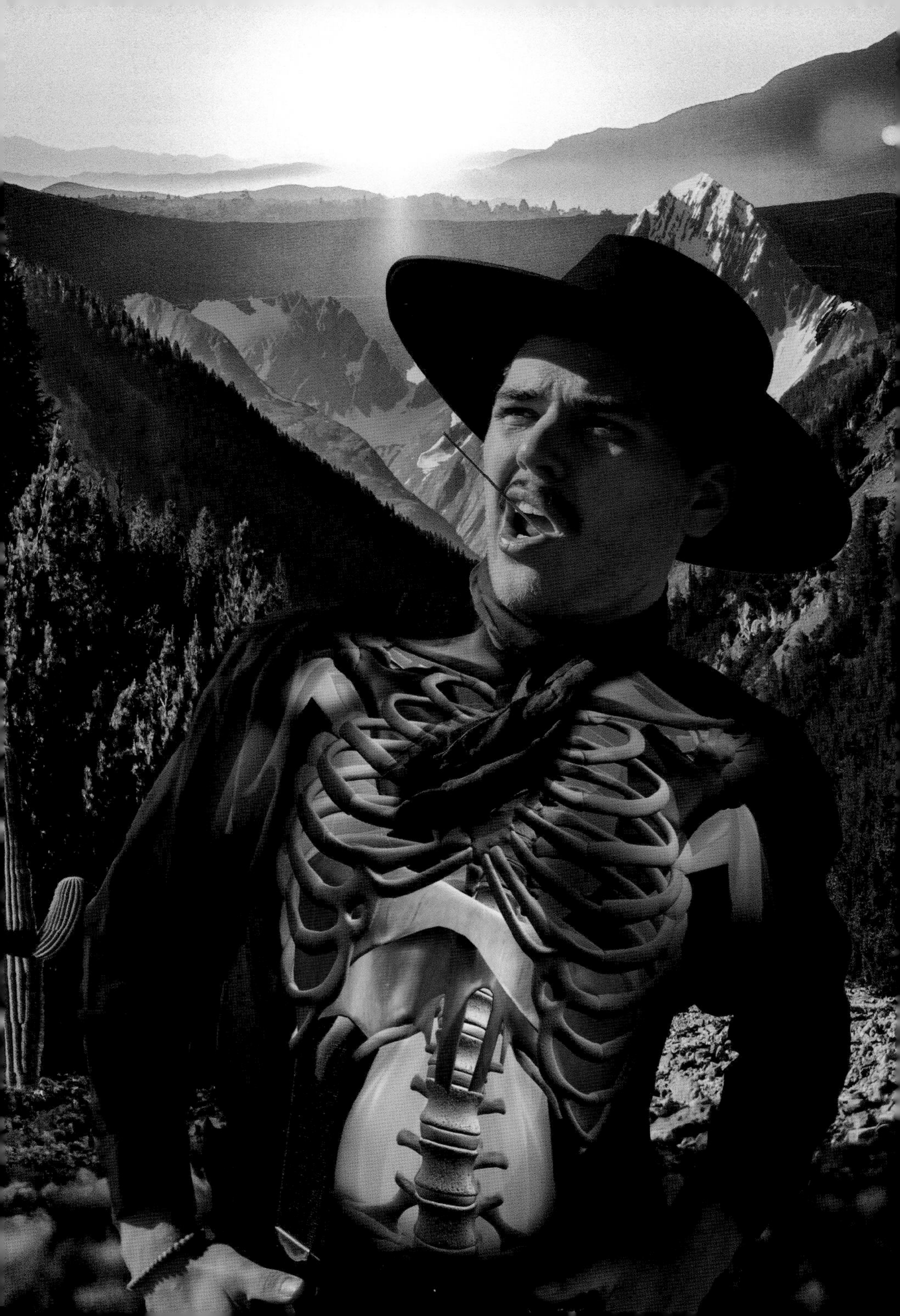

Breathing for singing

As a singer, it's important to understand that you can't feel your diaphragm or use it independently, it is involved in every breath you take

What is breathing for singing?

Because Mrs Romans, my intimidating, flame-haired biology teacher, had meticulously devoted her energies to teaching us the minutiae of the respiratory system, my twelve-year-old self was perplexed when the head of music insisted that we should 'breathe through our belly buttons' while singing. This has echoes in the common notion that we should be 'singing from our diaphragms'. Lots of singers have absolutely no idea what this means and I am not surprised. Although the diaphragm (a detailed explanation of which is coming up) is involved in building pressure in the abdomen for lifting, pushing and childbirth, its only job in breathing is to draw air into the lungs: beyond that, it has no other purpose. Essentially it is as impossible to 'sing from your diaphragm' as it is to 'breathe through your belly button'.

The issue here is in the terminology that is generally used to describe the sensation of 'abdominal' breathing. My music teacher was simply wording things in a way that she felt would be best understood by her young pupils. 'Abdominal', 'belly' or 'low' breathing is widely accepted as the most efficient way to breathe for singing. This is because it involves the ribs and diaphragm working together to increase the

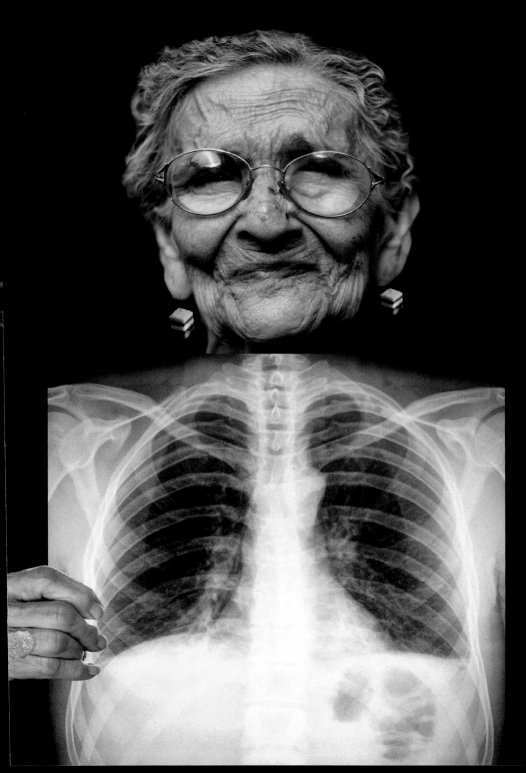

THE
DIAPHRAGM

Sternum   Diaphragm

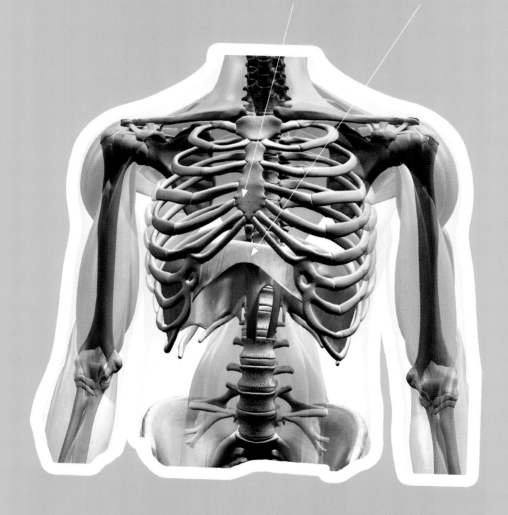

When you breathe in, the ribcage
expands and the diaphragm
flattens downward, drawing air
into the lungs like a bellows

volume of the chest cavity and, in order to maintain the same air pressure inside your body as that of the atmosphere outside, your body draws in as much air as it needs to fill that empty space. Basically, the larger the chest volume, the more air is drawn in to fill the lungs. Breathing 'high', also known as clavicular breathing, doesn't increase the volume of the chest cavity to the same extent and encourages inefficient, shallow breathing. The effort expended in high breathing is also likely to introduce tension into your neck and shoulders.

The great news is that you can learn to maximise your chest volume. Let me show you what abdominal breathing means in practice and you can develop your own descriptive terms that best fit the sensations you experience.

A word of warning: if you are not used to low breathing, you might feel light-headed, so if this happens take a moment to sit down and recalibrate.

Demystifying that diaphragm!

The diaphragm is a sheet of muscle and tendon that divides the chest cavity from the abdomen. It sits, dome-like in shape, up inside the ribcage, and is attached at the sternum and spine and around the bottom of the ribcage. When we breathe in, the ribcage automatically expands, which increases the volume of our chest cavity; when this happens, the diaphragm is activated to contract downward, flattening out, creating a vacuum to suck air into the lungs – a bit like a bellows. When we start to exhale, the diaphragm's job is over and it gradually returns to its dome-like position back up inside the ribcage, ready for the next inhalation.

These X-rays show the diaphragm as it contracts downward. The dark areas on either side of the spine are the lungs, which increase in size as the volume of the chest cavity increases. The side view shows how low the diaphragm descends at the back. Simply by imagining yourself breathing into the back of your ribcage – or down into your waist – more air is drawn into your lungs.

Put your hands across your belly and see how your abdomen moves outwards on the in-breath and returns to a flatter position on the out-breath. This is a consequence of the digestive system being pushed around by the downward movement of the diaphragm while breathing in, which explains why breathing can often feel uncomfortable after a big meal.

I hope you can see now how helpful it can be to imagine that you are drawing the air into the lower abdomen rather than into the chest while you are singing. Although it didn't make any sense to me as a schoolchild, I still imagine breathing in through my belly button. My old music teacher would be proud!

Breathing awareness exercise

Sit on a chair and lean forward, placing your forearms on your thighs. Imagine yourself breathing into your back and waist and feel a sense of the air filling your lower abdominal area, as if you are filling up a balloon. And yes, it can feel as if you are breathing in through your belly button! Be patient: you may have to do this several times before getting to grips with it. Give it a few minutes.

How much air do we need for singing?

If you have good posture and are breathing low, you will be taking in as as much air as you need for most singing tasks. There are some exceptions, like the punishingly long phrases and no-microphone rules of classical singing that may require more air, but in general you should trust yourself and resist the temptation to gulp in extra air. Even when

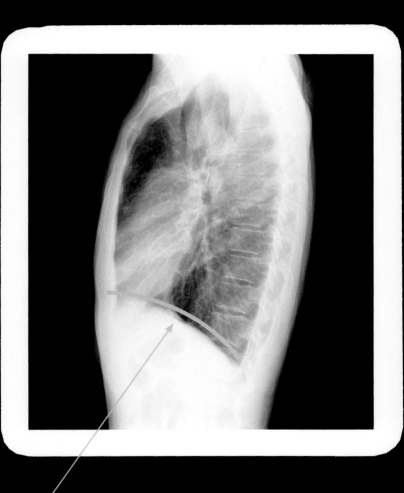

hragm

The diaphragm contracts much lower at the back. It can be helpful to imagine drawing air into the back of the ribcage

...EMENT

moves down it draws air into the lungs and pushes the digestive system out of the way

...age

Heart

Lungs

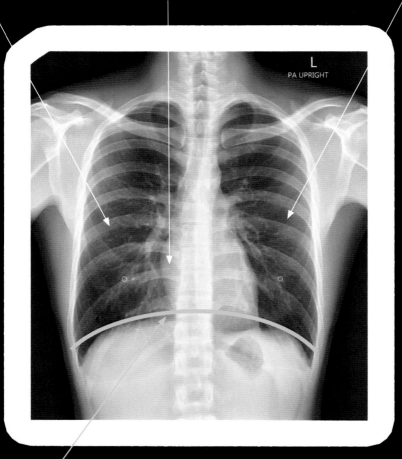

L
PA UPRIGHT

we feel that our lungs are empty we still have about twenty percent capacity remaining. The skill is to make the most of the air you have in your lungs and not to push it out by trying to sing loudly or straining for high notes.

Breathing in through the nose or mouth?

In singing it is best to breathe in through the mouth. Nose breathing is inefficient, requiring the closing of the lips or sealing off the airway to the mouth by dropping the soft palate.

When to take breaths while singing

A good rule of thumb is to breathe where it makes sense in the text. Acknowledging punctuation will help you; commas and full stops are indicators of some kind of change of direction. And never breathe in the middle of a word. If you are not sure about where the punctuation should fall, speak the lyrics out loud and feel where the pauses and changes of direction should naturally occur. There will be times when you struggle to sing through a phrase in one breath: in cases like this try to identify a moment where you could feasibly take an extra one. You will go out of tune if you try to sing without adequate breath. There will also be times when you can comfortably sing through two phrases in one breath, but I would advise against this if it compromises the meaning of the text.

Breathing: things to remember

- Posture check: tilting your sternum upward and tucking your tail bone under will make abdominal breathing feel easier.

- When you feel as if you are running out of air, resist the temptation to let your shoulders hunch forward or your sternum drop as this will collapse your ribcage and waste whatever air you do have left. So keep your chest open, with your shoulders rolled back and down.

- Allow the air to come out of your mouth, as opposed to pushing it out – the latter negatively impacts the quality of the sound and tuning. Inexperienced singers often push the air out at the beginning of phrases, which leaves them with insufficient air to get through to the end. Also, if you push the air out, the delicate edges of your vocal folds will start to complain about the force with which the air is passing through them and you may get a sore throat.

- The science shows us that the vocal folds prefer less air to go through them for high notes, so straining or pushing the air out of your mouth to reach high notes never works. I watched a demonstration of a very experienced singer belting out sustained high notes with a lit candle just in front of her mouth and the flame barely flickered. The higher you go in your range the less air you need. Recreating the sensation of complaining or whingeing about something will help shape the vocal tract in a way that makes singing these high notes effortless.

- Volume increases are not made by pushing the air out, but by managing your breath support and by making changes in the position of the tongue, jaw, lips and soft palate to highlight certain frequencies.

What is breath support?

Breath support is a term very commonly used in singing to describe how we employ muscles to stabilise our bodies while we sing. It is sometimes described as 'singing from the core'

Breath support is a term very commonly used in singing to describe how we employ muscles to stabilise our bodies, while we sing. It is sometimes described as 'singing from the core'.

The large muscles that we use for breathing influence the flow and pressure of the air as it goes through our vocal folds. An airstream that has too much or too little pressure behind it will not produce a good steady vibration in the vocal folds. The amount of air pressure you create is partly determined by the level of muscle engagement in your core. Core engagement will also make your breath last considerably longer. Without it, you will lose the air in your lungs very quickly, and sound wobbly and possibly rather breathy. You will also get a sense of singing from the throat, rather than the core, which is likely to introduce stress into the vocal tract. As you have no conscious control over the speed of your vibrating vocal folds, the necessity to use 'breath support' is absolutely crucial. Singers can learn to feel what's appropriate for different singing tasks: when you get it right, it makes singing feel fantastically easy.

Your vocal folds are open when breathing, to allow the air to enter the lungs, and need to come together to make sound. They work like a valve; putting a little bit of air pressure underneath draws the folds

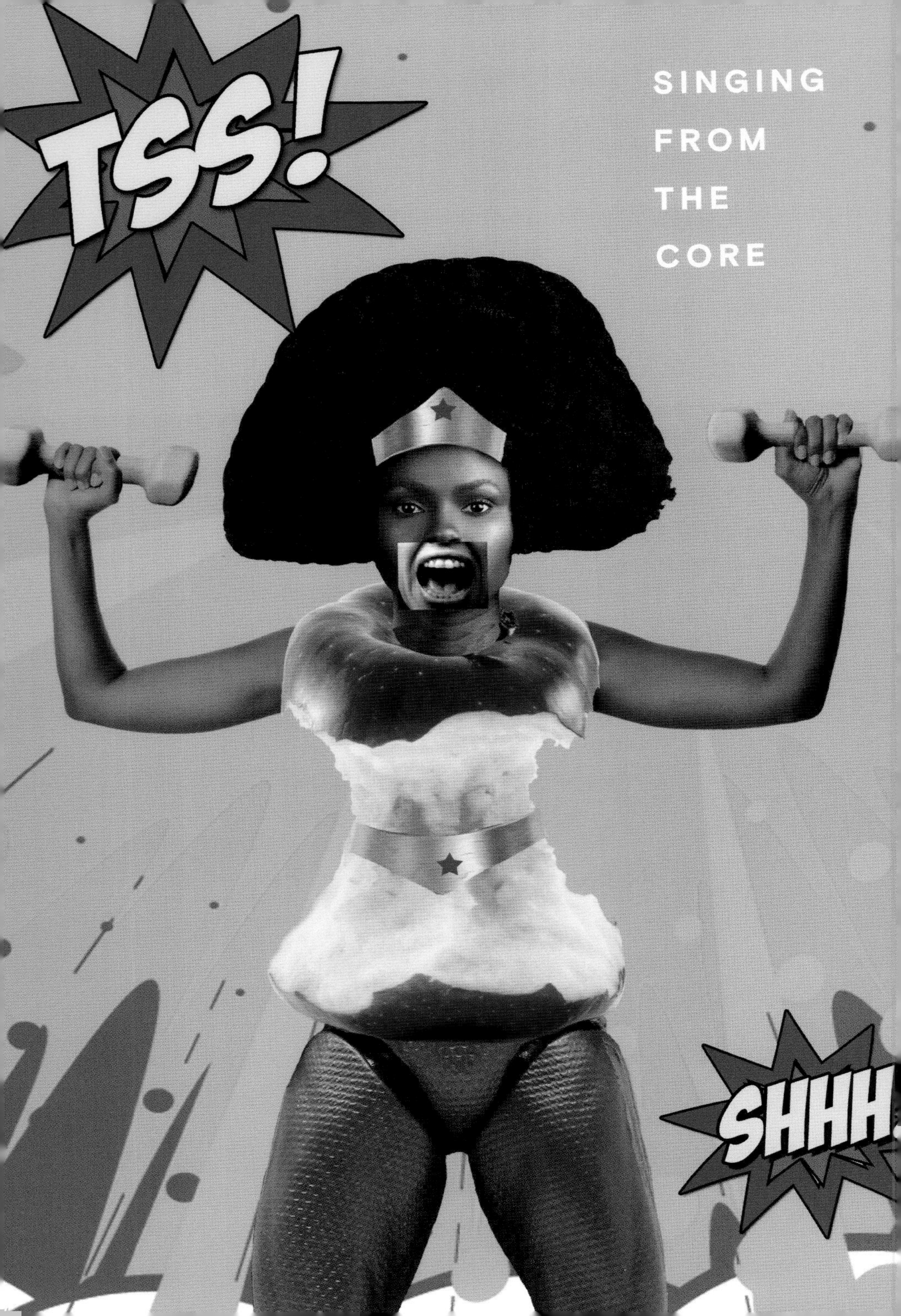
TSS!
SINGING FROM THE CORE
SHHH

together and initiates vibration. So the interaction of the breath with the vocal folds is important. There needs to be a balance. If you want to be really geeky, look up Bernoulli's principle on the inverse relationship between pressure and speed to understand how they are drawn together. If you have ever overtaken a lorry at high speed on the motorway or stood on the edge of the platform as a non-stopping train rushes past, you will have felt yourself being sucked towards the train or the lorry. It's that!

It is important to recognise that you only need breath support while you are singing, and that singing happens on the out-breath and not on the in-breath.

So this is what the cycle of breathing and breath support in singing should look like:

- Inhale through the mouth, imagining drawing the air down to the abdomen

- Engage the core muscles

- Set your throat to the emotional setting you want (page 34)

- Sing the phrase while maintaining core engagement

- Release the muscles

- Repeat

Here's a summary of **why we need breath support:**

· Allows the air in our lungs to last much, much longer

· Creates desirable pressure in our airstream, which is essential for producing good tone and singing tunefully

· Essential for good vocal health by eliminating the likelihood of strain in the throat

Breath support – how to do it

The **abdominal wall** and the **oblique muscles**, collectively known as **core muscles**, are the two principal sets of muscles used in breath support. The active engagement of these muscles will have a stabilising effect on the body during singing.

Finding and engaging the obliques

Place your hands on your waist with your thumbs facing forward and press into the soft flesh of your waist. Now laugh, cough very gently or pant and you should feel the oblique muscles engage. See if you can extend the length of the time you engage these muscles by saying TSS and holding the SS for a few seconds. Repeat this a few times and try to decrease the amount of air you use to make the SS sound. Your oblique muscles should work for you without any real effort. Do remember to relax the muscles when you breathe in. Repeat this a few times, until you feel confident that you can feel the obliques engaging under your thumbs while you are making sound.

Finding and engaging the abdominal wall

Using two fingers, find the soft fleshy spot just beneath your sternum.

MAIN MUSCLES
OF BREATH SUPPORT

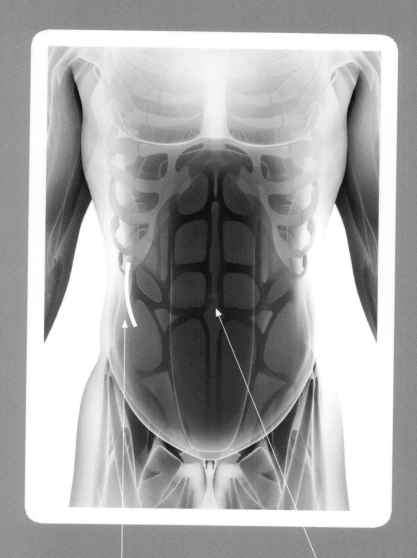

Oblique muscles   Abdominal wall

Now gently apply a little pressure through your fingers and cough, laugh or pant, and you will feel the engagement of the top of the abdominal wall. Move your fingers directly downward and do the same thing in a few spots all the way down your lower abdominal region. The whole length of the abdominal wall becomes engaged each time you cough, laugh or pant; it may feel as though you are pulling your abdominals in and up. See if you can extend the duration of the muscle engagement by saying TSS and holding the SS for a few seconds, just as you did when you were engaging your oblique muscles. Repeat this a few times and try to decrease the amount of air you use to make the SS sound.

By coughing, laughing and panting, you are engaging your obliques and abdominal wall muscles at the same time and when you do manage to do this while singing, you will be 'supporting your breath'. Hurray and congratulations! This is a huge achievement.

Engaging the core: further awareness exercise

This exercise in self-awareness will further develop your sense of engaging your oblique and abdominal muscles.

- Lie on your back on the floor with your knees bent or straight.

- Close your eyes and become aware of yourself breathing.

- Feel your ribcage expanding at the back and sides when you inhale.

- Place your hands on top of each other across your belly button.

- Feel your abdominal area rising as you breath in and dropping as you breathe out.

- Now breathe in and, as you breathe out, engage your core muscles by emitting a sustained TSS. You will feel the abdominal wall pull in a bit.

- Take another breath and repeat the cycle; you will notice that the core muscle engagement stops the abdominal area from quickly collapsing, as it descends much more slowly than it would without such engagement.

- Now see if you can maintain the engagement of those muscles while counting, or reciting the ABC. How far you can get without taking an in-breath? I hope you will see that your air goes a lot further than you might expect.

- Now try the same exercise singing a sustained VV on any comfortable note

- Now you are ready to do this exercise while standing up. Watch the hands on your belly rise on the in-breath and draw in on the out-breath.

Be reassured that while learning this skill takes a bit of effort, once you've got it it will come almost naturally. It takes practice and coordination, but eventually you will engage your support without giving it a second thought and will be able to instinctively feel how much stabilisation you need to apply, whatever you are singing.

Adding a few extras

There will be times when singing that you will feel the need for some extra help from your body. Adding ribcage and back stabilisation to your abdominal engagement can help when you are struggling with long phrases, rhythmic passages with limited opportunities to breathe, and challenging high notes.

ADDING A FEW EXTRAS

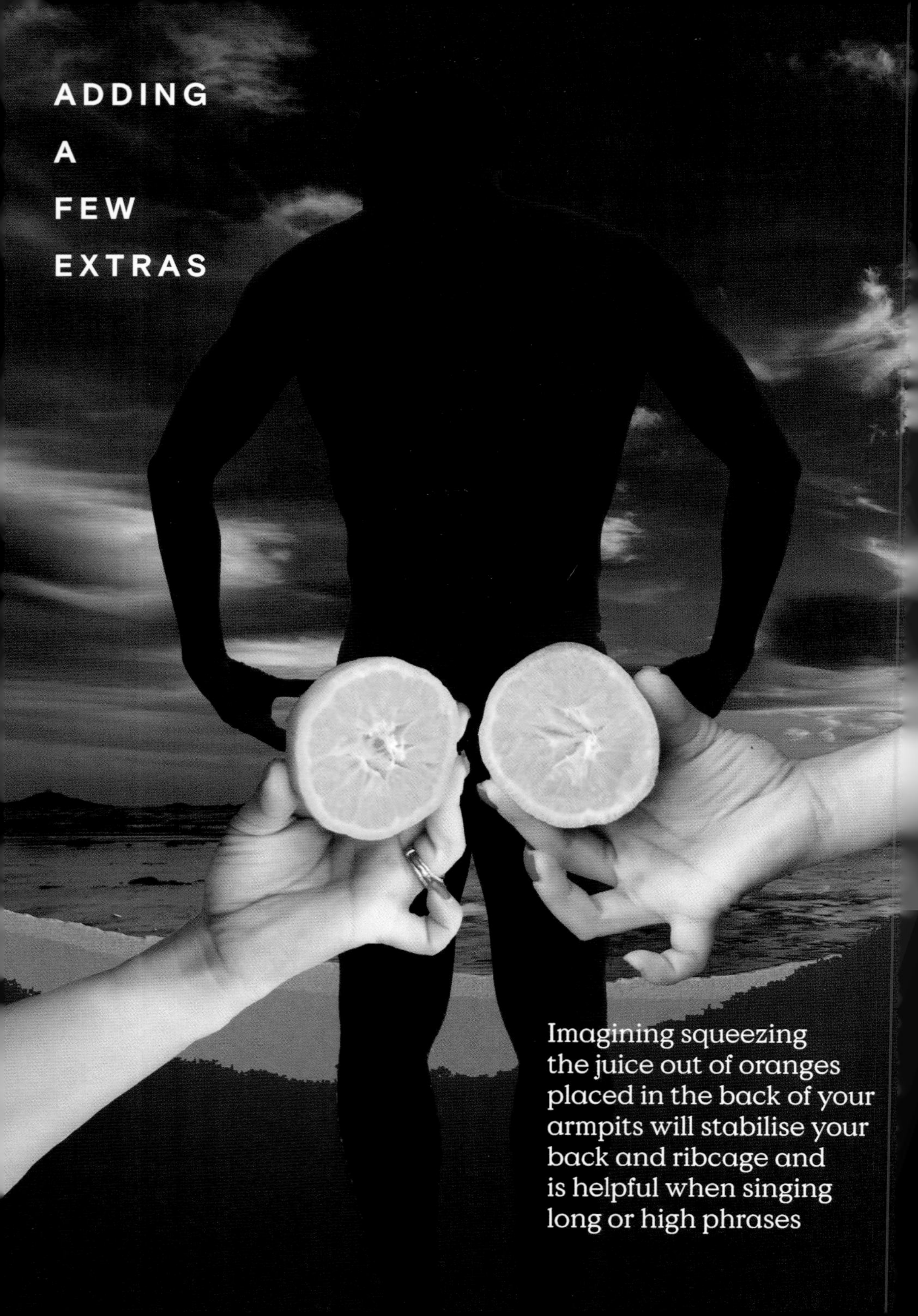

Imagining squeezing the juice out of oranges placed in the back of your armpits will stabilise your back and ribcage and is helpful when singing long or high phrases

Experiment with any of the following ideas and see which ones work best for you.

- During a challenging moment, roll your shoulders back and down, pulling your shoulder blades together and downward towards your waist. This stabilises your back and ribcage, giving a sense of lengthening down the back of the neck.

- Imagine a little orange in the back of each armpit and squeeze the juice out of them by pressing the insides of your arms against your ribcage – you will feel the large, flat lateral muscles in your back anchoring your waist and the back of your ribcage.

- An alternative to the 'oranges' is to imagine that you are at the gym and you are pulling a weighted bar down from above your head to slightly behind you, bringing your elbows to waist height and you will feel the same sense of anchoring the torso.

Fricative consonants

If you want to feel the connection between your support muscles and your voice, you need to get familiar with **fricative consonants**. You will already be using fricatives all the time in everyday speech; you just need to think about them in a new way.

A fricative sound is made when you force air through a narrow channel, which you create by placing two or more articulators (lips, teeth, tongue) together.

The following are known as **'unvoiced' fricative consonants**, as the only sound you will hear is the air passing through the small space:

- FF – formed by air flowing between the top front teeth when they are placed on the bottom lip

- SHHH – formed by air flowing between closed teeth and open lips

- TSS – formed by air flowing against the alveolar ridge (the front of the hard palate) and the teeth

- SS – formed by air flowing through a small gap between the roof of the mouth, the tongue and almost closed teeth

'Voiced' fricative consonants are created when your tongue is repositioned in order to add 'voice' to the sound:

- VV (like in the word 'very') – a similar set-up to FF (above) but requires you to reposition the back of your tongue to vocalise the sound, which turns it into VV

- ZZ (like in 'zebra') – similar to SS but requires you to vocalise the sound by moving the back of the tongue to morph SS into ZZ

- ZHUH (like 'treasure') – similar to SHHH but changing the position of the tongue, once again, vocalises the sound

FRICATIVE CONSONANTS

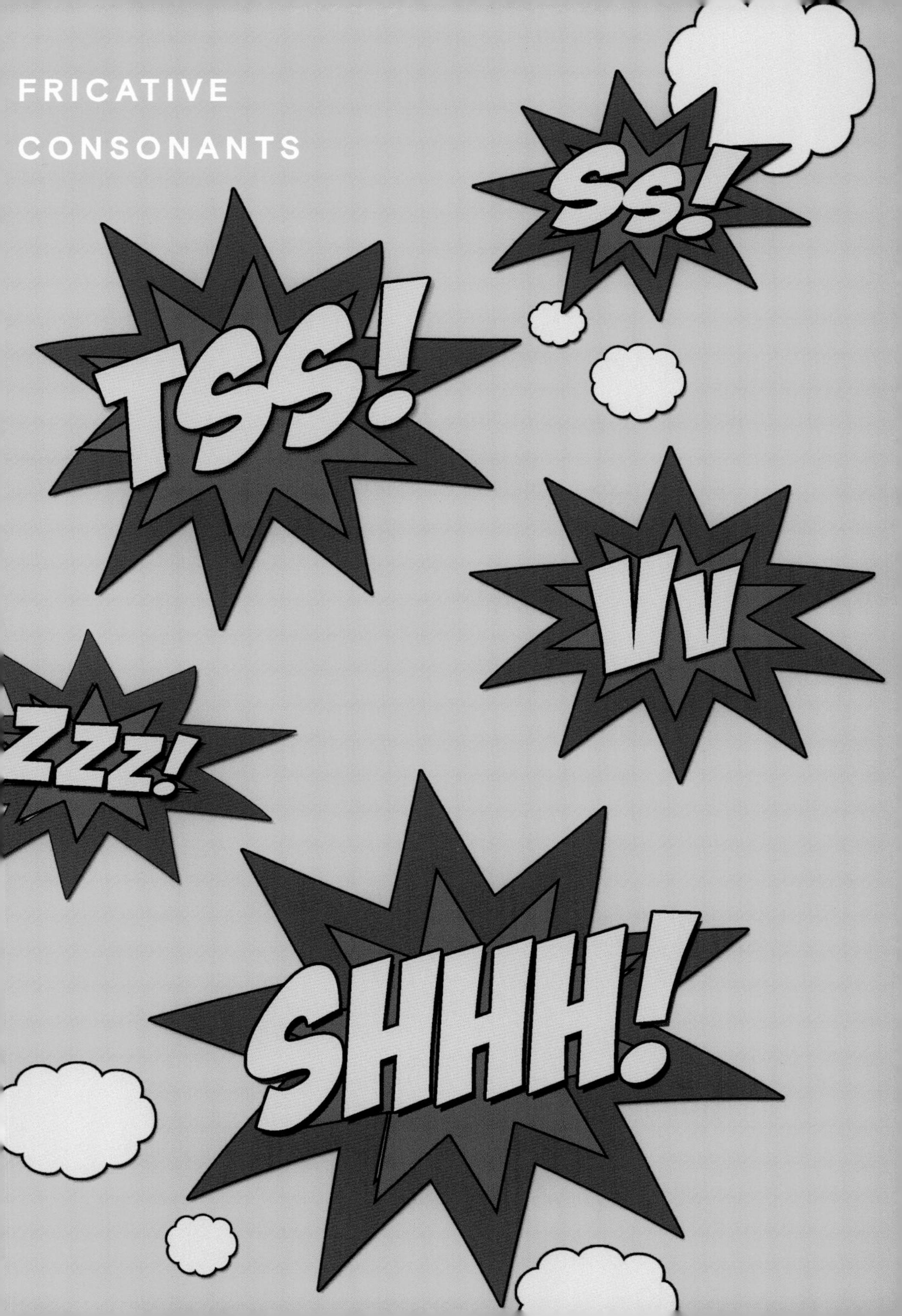
Ss!
TSS!
Vv
ZZZ!
SHHH!

Breath support exercises

Exercise one

- Standing up, check your posture and place your hands, thumbs forward, on your waist, pressing into the obliques.

- Sustain unvoiced fricatives (FF, SHHH, TSS, SS) for about four seconds each while becoming aware of the engagement with your core (use your thumbs to help you feel the muscles). Do this for a couple of minutes.

- Move on to the voiced fricatives VV and ZZ. Start by sustaining these sounds on any note that is comfortable, for about four seconds, and build up to sustaining the sound for an increasing number of counts.

- Sustain a voiced fricative for four counts and, on the same breath, continue maintaining your core muscle engagement for another four counts without making the fricative sound.

Exercise two

Sing 'Twinkle Twinkle, Little Star', replacing the words with VV while feeling your core muscles engaging under your thumbs at your waist.

Exercise three

Now we are going to sing the words of 'Twinkle Twinkle, Little Star' using the following cycle of breathing:

With relaxed abdominals, open your throat and inhale through your mouth

Engage the muscles by releasing TSS

Without taking a breath after the TSS, sing the phrase of the song:

Twinkle twinkle, little star

- Release the muscles

- Repeat

TSS... How I wonder what you are

- Release the muscles

- Repeat

TSS... Up above the sky so high

- Release the muscles

- Repeat

TSS... Like a diamond in the sky

- Release the muscles

- Repeat

TSS... Twinkle twinkle, little star

- Release the muscles

- Repeat

TSS... How I wonder what you are

Keep checking your posture throughout, ensuring that your sternum is lifted and your tail bone is tucked under. Make sure that when you are singing you are not pushing the air out of your mouth. If you are not sure whether you are doing this or not, try singing quietly and see how it feels. If your voice starts to wobble, you'll know something is not quite right and that you possibly need to use less air or perhaps adjust your level of breath support.

It might take several sing-throughs before you start to feel confident with this exercise but when you feel ready, you can start to omit the TSS and see if you can engage your abdominals without it. You should now be feeling a connection between your core and your voice. There should be no stress in your throat; the only effort should come from your core.

This is likely to feel physically demanding to start with, and you may even get some abdominal aching, but bear in mind that we often over-exert ourselves when we are learning something new. The amount of effort will eventually be minimal and your abdominal movement barely noticeable.

OPEN YOUR THROAT

As you breathe in, imagine your throat as a wide open tube that extends down to your abdomen drawing the air low into your belly

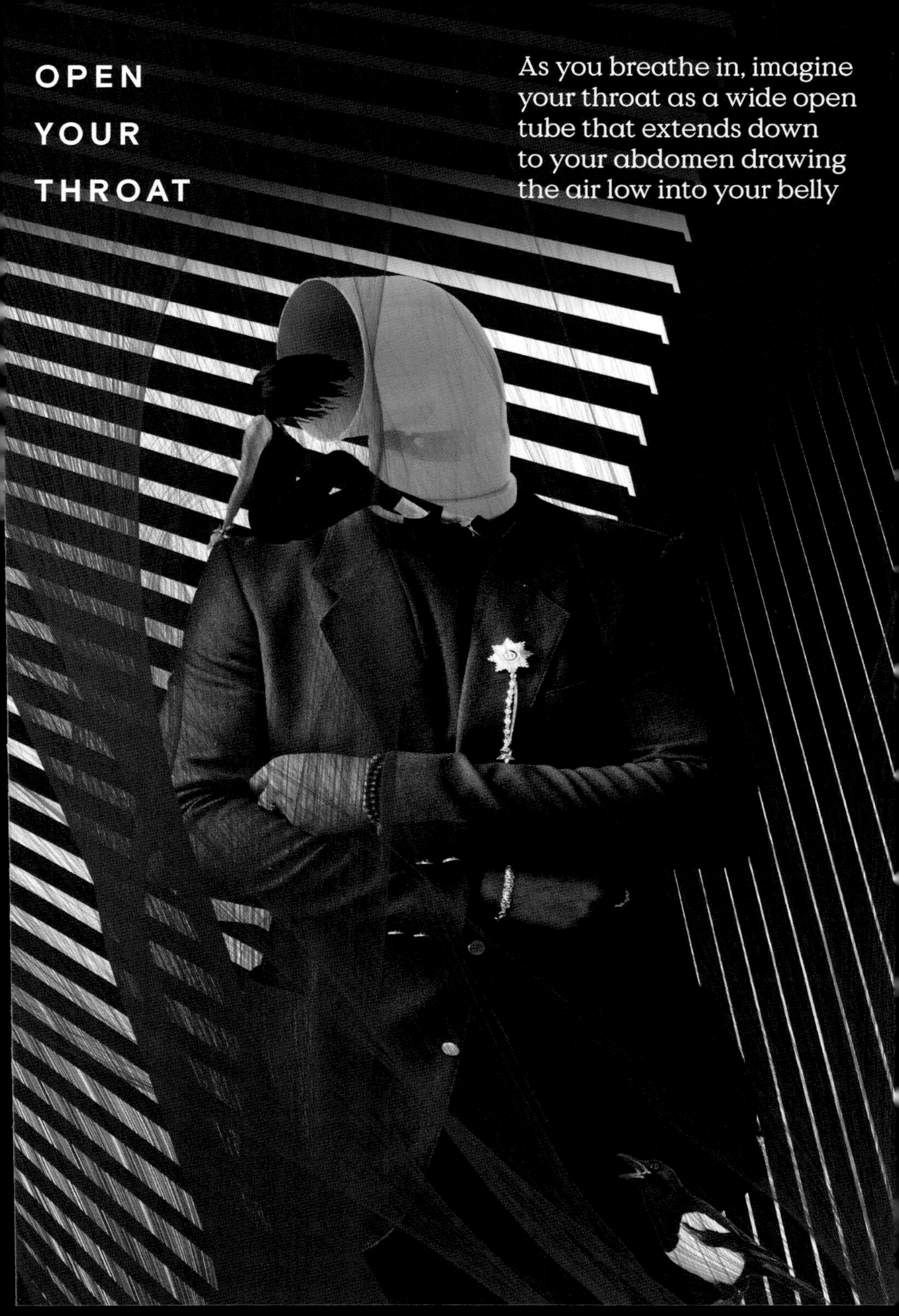

Troubleshooting your breath control

Not having enough air

Make sure that you are breathing in through your mouth. Check your posture, making sure that your sternum is lifted and that you are breathing low. If you can see your shoulders rising you are likely to be taking higher and more shallow breaths – remember that engaging your abdominal support muscles will allow your breath to last much longer. You might also be being overly ambitious about how long you think you should go without taking a breath, so try finding another moment in the phrase to take an extra one.

Going out of tune at the ends of phrases

It might be hard to detect unless you record yourself, but this is very common among new singers, for several reasons. It could be an indication that you are letting your breath support muscles relax before you have finished the phrase, so keep your fingers pressed into the upper abdominal wall just beneath your sternum and make sure the muscle engagement lasts throughout. Or you might be releasing too much air at the beginning of the phrase, which doesn't leave enough for you to get through to the end tunefully. Try starting the phrase at the same volume and with the same intensity that you will use for the rest of it.

Singing too loudly

Are you forcing the air through your vocal folds? If you're finding that you are running out of breath, try experimenting with your volume.

How do you know if you are not supporting?

When you are not singing from your core, you will feel and hear a disconnect between your voice and your breath, a sense of being untethered. This might induce a wobble in your voice and you may feel as if you are singing from your throat. If this happens, stop and check your posture, breathe low into your abdominals (through the belly button!), remind yourself of the sensation of abdominal engagement by using an unvoiced fricative such as TSS or SHHH, and start again. It can also be helpful to replace the words of the song by singing a voiced fricative instead, such as VV, to help you regain the sense of connection between your voice and your breath.

I appreciate that concepts like these may seem abstract when read as text in a book, but just give it a go – when it all falls into place you will feel the vocal freedom that breath support allows and know that the effort of learning was worthwhile. Remember when you learned to ride a bike and kept falling off, and then occasionally you found your balance, until eventually you found you could ride without a second thought? That!

CHAPTER

EIGHT

WARMING

UP

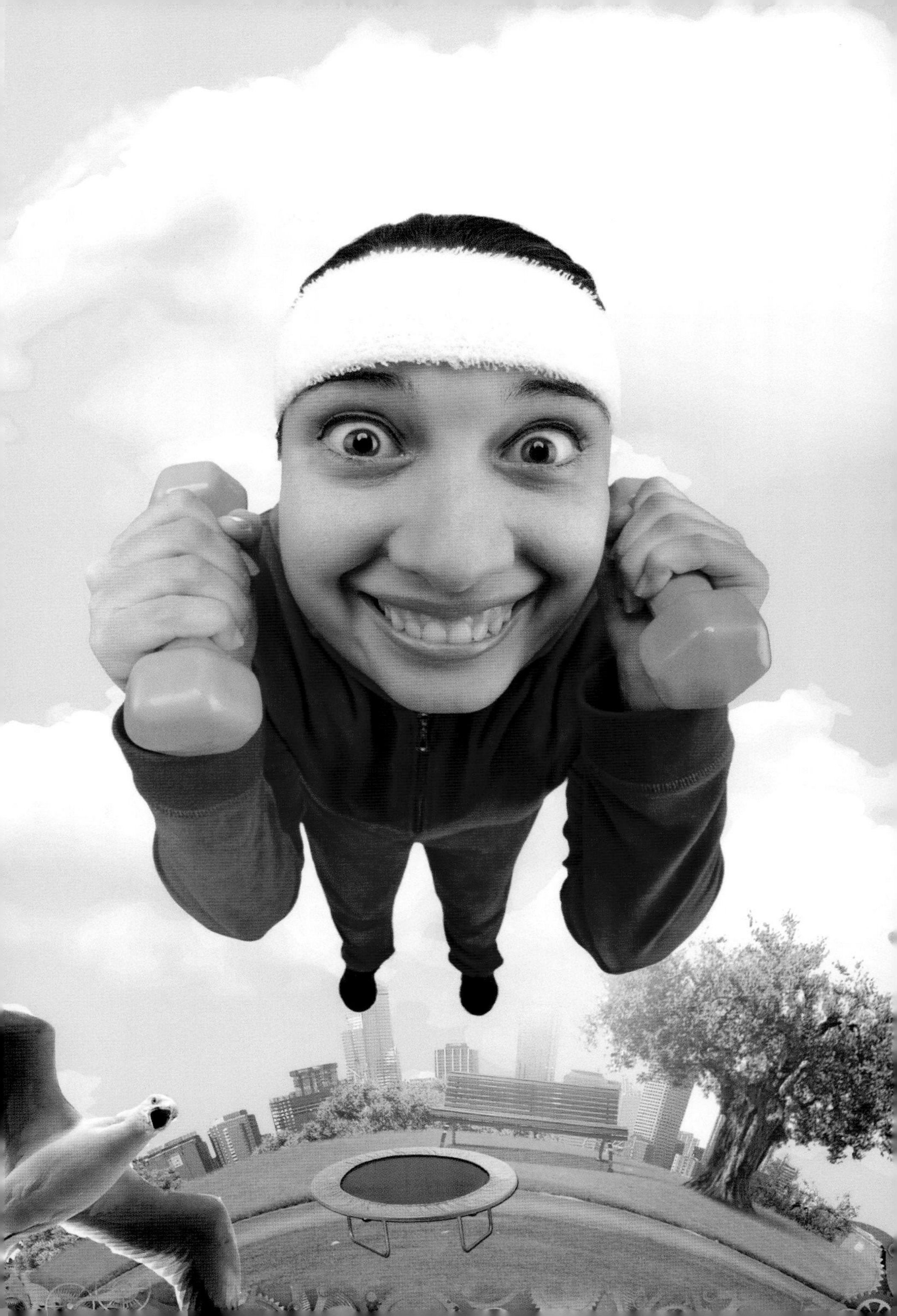

Warming up

As with any physical activity, your singing muscles need to be warm and oxygenated to be able to work at their best

Does warming up really make a difference?

Yes! As with any physical activity, your singing muscles need to be warm and oxygenated to be able to work at their best and to prevent vocal damage. A ballet dancer with the muscular capability to fall into splits knows only too well that such demands made on cold muscles may result in injury. Comfortable singing requires stamina, flexibility and coordination, all of which involve the repetitive fine-tuning and toning of muscle groups.

A warm-up should serve as an awakening, a sense of mental and physical reconnection with the large muscles used for posture and abdominal breathing and the smaller ones that work so miraculously to create sound. A good warm-up will release real-life-generated tension in the shoulders, neck and jaw. It is so much easier and more pleasurable to sing with a voice that has been warmed up.

A vocal warm-up is not the same as vocal 'exercises', which are specific either to the music you are learning or to your needs as a singer. It's really worth knowing this, as I have come across singers who use scales to warm up with, which is vocally demanding and unwise to do on a cold set of muscles.

Nor is warming up about making beautiful sounds or hitting accurate notes. It's more about feeling yourself making sounds.

What should be included in a warm-up?

Your vocal warm-up should always include sirens and trills:

Sirens

Sirening is the act of gliding smoothly up and down through consecutive notes, rather like the sound of an air-raid siren, and is very popular as a warm-up tool for singers. The sense of gliding is very different to singing the individual notes of a scale, which can be hard work on the vocal tract. Sirening gets the micro-muscles of your larynx warmed up and helps iron out the vocal 'breaks' that can happen to all singers as they change gear between ranges of low notes and ranges of high notes. As you warm up on a siren, increase the distance between your lowest note and your highest. You can siren on all kinds of sounds, including trills.

Trills

Trills are alternating notes produced very quickly, the most common of which are lip trills and tongue trills.

Lip trills are achieved by blowing air through loosely closed lips causing them to vibrate. This can sound like the put-put-put of the small engine of a motorbike or motorboat and is similar to blowing a raspberry. You will need good breath support for lip trills.

Tongue trills involve a series of rolled Rs. Think of the R sound in the Spanish word 'ARRIBA!' Practise using a tongue trill on a siren. It's my personal go-to warm-up: I absolutely love it and think it's one of the best warm-ups there is.

Lots of people struggle with lip and tongue trills, so go easy and be patient. You will almost certainly need to practise tongue and lip trills on one note before you attempt to glide up and down your range.

Your daily warm-up

I have prepared this daily warm-up that you can do for five to twenty minutes a day, depending on your needs and schedule. Five minutes a day in the shower will start you building flexibility and stamina and 'awaken' your voice, ready for your day ahead. Fifteen to twenty minutes will warm your voice up thoroughly before singing and accelerate your long-term development. However long you spend, doing something every day is better than embarking on a singing binge every ten days.

It's worth mentioning that warming up or practising your singing over the noise of a car engine can tempt you into 'pushing' to hear yourself, which may give you a sore throat.

I would suggest aiming for a minimum of one minute of repetitions for each of the following exercises. I have laid them out in an order that should warm you up methodically.

If anything feels uncomfortable, stop. Take a step back, check your posture and try laughing, which is a great way to alleviate physical stress in the throat. Nothing should ever hurt in singing; if it does, stop straight away and seek professional advice.

- **Start by raising your temperature** If you are physically cold when you want to sing, increase your body temperature and pulse rate with low-impact whole body movements (I think the movements of the 'Hokey Cokey' are pretty good, but try getting creative with your own version).

- **Stretch the back and sides of your neck** Use the weight of your head to drop it on to your chest and to each side without letting your shoulders collapse.

- **Check your posture in a mirror** Make sure that your shoulders are down and open, the back of your neck feels long and you are not arching your back.

- **Become aware of low breathing and breath support** Place your hands on your waist, thumbs forward, pressing into your oblique muscles. Breathe in through your nose and feel your oblique muscles engage under your thumbs while you release a TSS sound. Repeat several times. Drop your hands from your waist and place two fingers in the soft tissue just below the sternum, and this time feel the abdominal wall engage as you release your breath on TSS. Repeat several times.

- **Sirens** The following are fantastic warm-ups that I would recommend always including. Repeat the previous exercise but now breathe in through your mouth and, instead of TSS on the out-breath, start with the voiced fricative VV, followed by ZHUH. Start on one note before moving on to small sirens of about three notes, gradually increasing the range between the lowest and highest notes. Remember to check that your obliques and abdominal wall are engaged by placing your thumbs on your waist and then two fingers under your sternum. These are principal stabilisers and need to be engaged during singing and relaxed on the inhalation.

- **Poke your tongue out of your mouth** Feel as if you are stretching it out of your throat rather than pushing it out of your mouth. Hold for a few seconds and bring it back in to a relaxed position, and then do the same twice more. Give your tongue a good workout by using it to clean your teeth and to draw circles inside your cheeks.

- **Try some loose-jaw chewing with your mouth closed and open** If you think you have jaw tension, give your jaw and the chewing muscles in your cheeks a massage.

- **Mumming** Allow your jaw to relax and maintain a finger-width distance (0.5–1cm) between your upper and lower molars. Without changing the position of your jaw, gently close your lips and start to hum on a medium to low note. Find the lip position that generates the most vibration while humming. When you feel comfortable, begin with small sirens, being careful not to lose that vibration. If you do lose it, don't go so high.

- **NG** On any medium low note, sing the word 'sing' and sustain the NG. Without letting go of the sense of relaxation you found in the mumming warm-up, begin to siren on the NG, going a bit higher and a bit lower on each one.

- **Lip trills** Some singers find it easier to start on a low to medium note for this. Make sure your jaw is loose and your lips are relaxed and begin to blow a steady stream of raspberries. When you are confident with sustaining a lip trill on a single note, start doing small sirens; to do this you will need to have your breath support in place.

- **Tongue trills** My personal favourite! A very effective warm-up. Using the rolled RR sound in 'ARRIBA!' do exactly as you did with the lip trills; start by sustaining one note and then gradually introduce a siren. If you struggle with this, take comfort from

knowing that lots of other people do too, and the answer is to be
patient and to practise little and often.

Warming down

After an intense period of any type of physical activity, it's good
practice to spend a bit of time resetting your muscles to their neutral
state. In singing, your vocal tract is likely to have been held in a higher
(sometimes lower) position than is required for speaking, and all those
micro-muscles will have been very busy shaping it to accommodate the
different notes. You will have been using your core muscles for breath
support and the general excitement of singing is in itself physically
exerting. Post-singing warming down will reduce muscle stiffness and
help you regain and improve your flexibility and stamina.

> After an intense period of physical
> activity, it's good practice to spend
> a bit of time resetting your muscles

As little as five minutes will make a difference to how quickly your voice
recovers and will keep you in good vocal health. Here are a few ideas
that you can repeat for a minute or so each:

- **Vocal fry or creak** This is a low, creaking sound, much like a
spooky door opening in a cartoon. In singing, it is the most
commonly used intervention to eliminate muscle tension in your
throat. Starting on a medium-high pitch, glide down in a sighed
AH to a relatively low note in your range and sustain a creaking
sound on an OH or AH. It feels great. If you can't get it straight
away, try adjusting your lip shape or use a lower note.

- **Voiced fricatives** Pick a medium-low note that feels comfortable and sustain a VV sound.

- **Straws** With your lips acting as a seal around the top of a regular, medium-width straw, blow into a bottle of water. (You are less likely to get splashed with a bottle than a glass.) You are aiming to sustain a steady stream of bubbles. It doesn't matter how full the bottle is; what makes the difference to the exercise is the depth and angle at which you drop your straw into the water. Try tilting the bottle to give you better neck posture and experiment with the depth of your straw. The deeper you go, the harder you will have to blow and the more you will feel the sensation of back pressure in the mouth and throat. You can do this at any time you feel your voice is getting tired. In fact, anyone who uses their voice professionally (teachers, for example) can benefit from the soothing and therapeutic effects of this exercise. You will have to experiment with straws of different widths and lengths to find one that suits your personal needs. It's worth considering a reusable singer's straw, as these come with different gauges for different vocal tasks.

CHAPTER NINE

LEARNING FROM YOUR FAVOURITE SINGERS

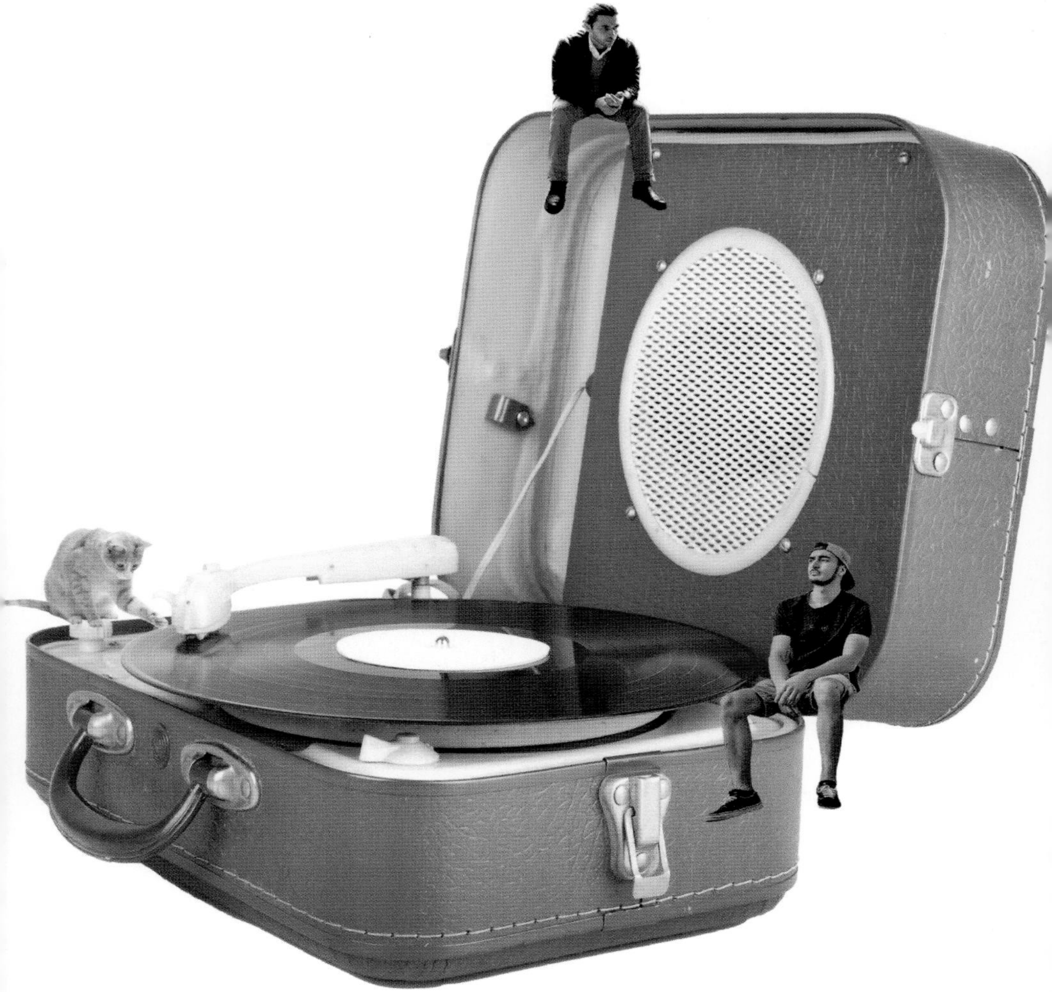

Learning from your favourite singers

Learning how to model other singers will fast-forward your progress

I am not suggesting you should surrender your vocal authenticity in favour of mimicry, but I am advocating this as a good way of learning and developing self-awareness. For example, if you try to model Cher singing 'If I Could Turn Back Time' you will soon find that her distinctive sound is made by shaping her tongue into an American R (say 'red' in a Deep Southern accent and feel the sensation of your tongue pulling backward). Celine Dion is a master of breathy sobbing and uses a distinct vibrato (a deliberate and attractive wobble) in her sound. That sobbing position in your throat can be very helpful – if you listen to the Three Tenors you will detect an element of sobbing in their singing, particularly on higher notes.

The Bee Gees, who developed an instantly recognisable sound by using hyper-falsetto (very high and breathy), sold hundred of millions of records despite the unusual nature of their vocals. Kate Bush uses a similar vocal set-up in some of her songs. If you can model this sound you will feel the sensation of your vocal-tract shaping for your higher registers, which is invaluable for all kinds of singing. The distinctive sound made by the French singer Edith Piaf is rich in resonance and vibrato. Barry White's ability to speak in an insanely erotic bass voice comes from shaping his vocal tract to exploit the last drop of velvety allure. These are pretty extreme stylists, but you can learn something from them all.

As a guest on the Graham Norton chat show, the accomplished jazz singer Michael Bublé explained how he uses modelling – jokily referring to it as stealing – as a way to develop detail in his performance. He then proceeded to do wonderful impressions of Dean Martin and his distinctive 'low epiglottis', which might also be called a low larynx; Elvis and his vibrato; and Frank Sinatra, who had a love affair with vowels. Listen to Frank himself, and you will hear that he does indeed slam those vowels. Jessie J, meanwhile, openly states that her exceptional ability to riff is the outcome of hundreds of hours spent modelling her idols.

If you can mimic a particular singer's vocal set-up, try and analyse what you are doing to the point that you can retain that physical memory and implement it in some way into your own singing.

How to model

Listening and modelling are skills that are developed with lots of practice, so don't be hard on yourself if you struggle to work out what a singer is doing. I have spent time analysing performances with other experienced teachers and we often have conflicting opinions on how the singer is producing their sound. Without X-ray vision we can never really know what's going on inside a singer's vocal tract, but we can have a pretty good guess by modelling it ourselves.

When aiming to model a singer, bear in mind that live performances are likely to produce more interesting results than pre-recorded tracks, which will have received phonic airbrushing and not be a genuine representation of the voice. While singing, pay attention to the detail in the following: what is the position of your tongue (high, low, flat, forward, backward?), and what does the space in your throat feel like (wide, small, taut, low, flat?). If you can see the singer, note carefully what they are doing with their lips (wide, puckered, snarled, circular, neutral?), their jaw (how wide?) and their face (lifting cheekbones, frowning, smiling?), and how they are standing and breathing. These will all be good indicators as to how they are producing their sound.

If you watch the classical singer Cecilia Bartoli you will see that in addition to pulling strange faces, she pouts her lips significantly. When I tried this, I felt an instant and positive change in the quality of my sound and now use this as a technique for certain styles of singing.

Another good tip is to listen to several different versions of one song and pinpoint how each artist employs different strategies to take creative ownership of their performance. Highly covered popular songs that would be worth looking up include 'Fever', 'Yesterday', 'My Way', 'Imagine', 'Somewhere over the Rainbow' and Leonard Cohen's 'Hallelujah'.

Once you have begun to model the sound, start to identify the ingredients in the performance itself, such as the effect of volume changes, whether the singer sustains their vowels and how they employ their diction. Can you hear any vibrato? What about their creative choice for the quality of the sound – breathy, gravelly, twangy, dark or bright? – and how does that affect the mood of the piece? Great performers often change the quality of the sound they make several times in one song. It is these details that make artists stand out and allow audiences to emotionally engage with the songs they are singing.

There are lots of fantastic singers for you to draw inspiration from, from across all styles and decades. You can learn from all of them, the good ones and the not-so-good ones; check out Florence Foster Jenkins's 'Queen of the Night' aria from The Magic Flute, which is so legendary that they made a film about her. You should be able to hear the lack of connection between her voice and her breath. She must have been permanently exhausted!

CHAPTER

TEN

VOCAL

HEALTH

HEALTH
Organics
vocal nourisher

Vocal Health

Learning how to use
straws will help reduce
stress in the vocal tract –
highly recommended!

The dos and don'ts

- **Do drink plenty of water** Hydration is important in voice care because vocal folds dry out quickly and they need to be well lubricated to function efficiently. As it is not possible to apply water directly to the folds (you would cough), you need to make sure that you are sufficiently hydrated in advance of singing. There is so much contradictory advice on how much water we should be drinking that I will leave it to you to decide what feels like the right amount for you. Drinking room-temperature water thins mucus, which reduces the need to clear your throat. Be aware that decongestants and expectorants can have a drying effect on the vocal folds.

- **Do steam (highly recommended)** This is one of the best things you can do for your voice. Cover your head with a towel and lean over a bowl of hot water, or buy a steam inhaler cup that you can safely fill with just-boiled water and place your nose and mouth over the opening. The steam travels directly to your vocal folds and the lubricating effects are immediate.

- **Do sleep well** I know it's pretty obvious but there is no doubt that we need our sleep to recharge and repair. Without enough quality sleep, efficient brain function is compromised and muscles get more easily fatigued.

- **Do be aware of your voice, and listen out for changes** Our voices are in a perpetual state of evolution as we go through life, so certain gradual changes in tone are inevitable. However, sudden inexplicable changes in the quality of your voice are not normal and should be properly investigated.

- **Do warm up before extensive voice use** Warm, oxygenated muscles work much better than cold ones and are less likely to strain.

- **Do warm down after extensive voice use** Hard-working muscles in any part of the body need to be released and reset.

- **Do release stress in the jaw and neck before singing** Tension anywhere around the vocal tract will impact the quality of the sound and may lead to a sore throat or injury.

- **Do use a straw to blow bubbles into water** The back pressure created by the blowing (page 114) has a soothing effect on the vocal folds.

- **Do be aware of what you eat** It is well known that certain foods can cause excessive throat clearing but I want to avoid giving a list of these as we are all affected by different things in different ways. My advice is to keep a note of the foods that irritate your throat and to avoid eating them before singing. Personally, I have learned not to consume spicy foods, orange juice and chocolate before I sing.

- **Do watch out for laryngopharyngeal reflux** This occurs when acid from the stomach travels all the way up the oesophagus and spills into the back of the throat and on to the vocal folds. It is a really unpleasant condition that can be abrasive to the throat and make singing difficult. Symptoms are variable and often sufferers don't know they have it. If you regularly wake up with a sore throat, have sudden coughing or choking spasms, a lump in your throat or a bilious taste at the back of your mouth, or are frequently clearing your throat, it might be worth chatting to a doctor who can refer you to an ENT (ear, nose and throat) consultant. It is a treatable condition, so it's worth getting it checked out. Sleeping in a more upright position or on your side and taking alginates can help alleviate the symptoms.

- **Don't hold a sneeze back** Holding in a sneeze can lead to eardrum ruptures as well as ruptures in the vocal tract.

- **Don't grunt when you lift weights or play tennis, or vocalise when you strain** These can cause similar problems to holding back a sneeze.

- **Don't shout** Shouting can be traumatic for your vocal folds, which don't like having air forced through them.

- **Don't whisper** Whispering can be as damaging as shouting, for the same reason.

- **Don't persistently clear your throat** The vocal folds won't like it and may swell or get irritated.

- **Don't cough aggressively** It is extremely traumatic for the vocal folds and can rupture them, resulting in voice loss.

- **Don't continue to use your voice when you have a sore throat**
  It is possible to sing through a cold without doing any damage, as long as you don't have a sore throat or a cough or keep having to clear your throat. Pushing your voice under these conditions may cause the vocal folds to swell up and give you laryngitis. If you experience vocal problems for more than 3-weeks, you should visit your GP.

CHAPTER ELEVEN

HOW TO LEARN AND PERFORM A SONG

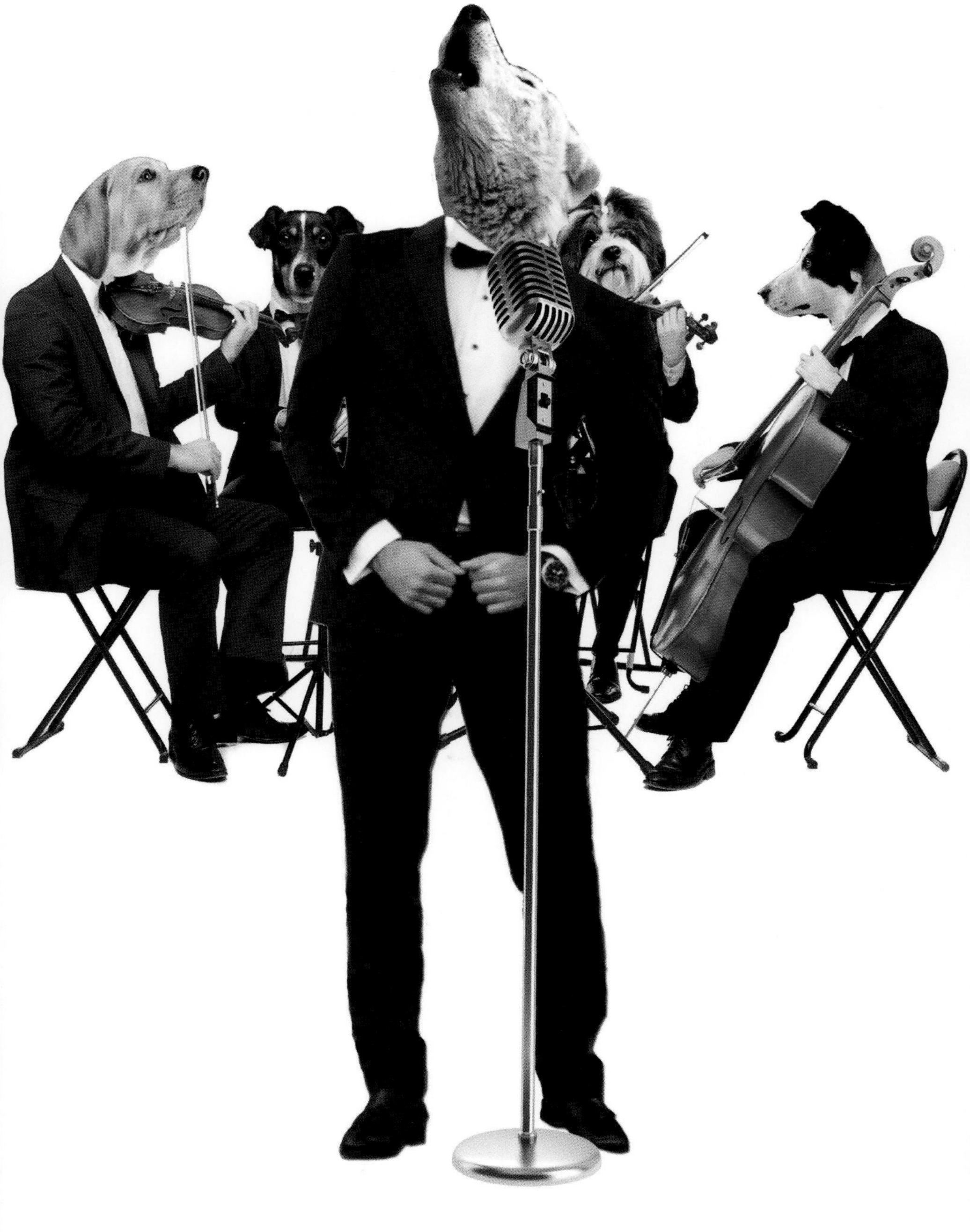

How to learn and perform a song

Technique and artistry must coexist; one without the other will lead to a disappointing outcome

You've been working really hard, so here's the fun stuff. You are ready to sing an actual song!

While technique (posture, breath support and vocal-tract shaping) is absolutely vital for good sound production, artistry is just as important. By this I mean the use of dynamics, phrasing and how you use your voice to express the narrative of a song. A singer who impresses with their agility, stamina and range is not necessarily the one who inspires or stirs minds and hearts. That said, one who sings with poor tone and bad tuning is not likely to win the minds and hearts of an audience either!

I have included lots of technical tips and ideas on artistry that you will be able to try out in a specially prepared song at the end of the chapter.

Where to start – choosing a song

Pick a song that you really like and are reasonably familiar with, and if possible, listen to several artists performing it. Feel free to be impressed by the artists you admire and learn as much as possible from them by modelling, but don't try to sound like them; their voice and their interpretation is uniquely theirs and you will be denying yourself the opportunity to find your own voice.

Start with a song that is relatively straightforward and isn't too high or too low. A little bit outside your comfort zone is fine! Then search for an online karaoke backing track that displays the lyrics.

It's worth noting that it can be challenging for a woman to sing a song made famous by a male singer, as the range of notes will often be too high or too low. This is because women generally sing an octave (8-notes) above the average male voice, so a man singing high or low in his range will make it very high or extremely low in a woman's voice. The same applies to men singing women's songs. There may be several versions of your chosen song in different keys, so have a hunt around.

Steps to learning and performing your song

Learning a song is a layering process and being methodical in the early stages will pay off.

Lyrics

Songs are stories told through music, so the lyrics really matter. However well you already know the song, start the learning process by reading the lyrics silently to yourself, as if they were text in a book, avoiding the temptation to emphasise rhymes or to add a rhythmic pulse. This takes a bit of practice.

Punctuation helps to highlight shifts in direction; observing commas and full stops, no matter how insignificant they seem, will help you make sense of the narrative and they should be acknowledged in the way you sing the song. Having no punctuation or incorrect punctuation can drastically alter the meaning of a phrase:

A woman without her man is nothing.

A woman: without her, man is nothing!

If there is no punctuation marked on your text, put some in!

Now read the lyrics out loud, still without adding your own rhymes or rhythm, and emphasise the key words in each phrase. Notice how changing the emphasis can disrupt or solidify a meaning.

It sounds horribly OTT and a touch embarrassing, but reading the words to your own reflection in the mirror, as if this might be the very person you are singing to, can help give a context.

Now it's time to consider what tone of voice the lyrics need for the meaning of the story to be conveyed clearly.

Science shows us that emotional states can alter the shape of our vocal tracts and how we engage our vocal folds, resulting in a shift in sound quality. For example, expressions of joy can often result in a higher pitch frequency and a brighter or breathier quality of sound (think of cooing over a puppy), while irritation can produce a more 'twangy' quality. We tried this idea out in the 'Happy Birthday' exercise (page 34), demonstrating that you can learn to switch on these vocal settings by triggering the relevant emotion (acting!). This makes it possible to set up your throat ready to produce a sound that reflects the right mood.

Sum up the meaning of your chosen song in a descriptive phrase and then write a few words on a card that reflect the song's emotional states. This creates a kind of mood board that will really help you prepare your body for singing that particular song well.

Once you have a grasp of the text, you need to make sure that you know how those words work with the music.

Learning the tune

There is a misconception that you need to be able to read sheet music in order to be able to sing well. This is absolutely not the case. All you need is access to the lyrics and a recording of someone singing the song you would like to learn. I can read sheet music but often don't have the right music to hand, so in those instances I mark up a lyric sheet with all the information I need to perform a song. It's fantastically helpful and really speeds up the learning process. Even if you think you know your chosen song well, it's still worth the effort to listen to a recording and check; there is normally one troublesome section in every song that can be sorted out by seeing which words are emphasised.

If you want to help yourself remember the tune, it can be useful to print out the lyrics and add an arrow above key words to indicate if they go up or down or if they stay on the same note as the previous word. Where are the long notes? Make sure you mark them in and sustain them when you come to sing the song.

You'll occasionally have trouble feeling the musical shape of a phrase and be left wondering why there seem to be too many words for the amount of music! Listen to the phrase a few times being sung by a singer you like and take a moment to work out where the tune emphasises a particular word and underline it. Now try singing it yourself but over-emphasising that key word until it starts to slot into the rhythm of the phrase, and then start to build in the other words around it. It is perfectly normal to have to break things down like this, even for experienced singers.

IMAGINE THE SOUND TRAVELLING FORWARD
SING TO A SPOT
DIRECTLY IN FRONT OF YOU

Bars and beats

In the same way that kilometres can be broken down into metres, centimetres and millimetres, all music is measured in units called 'bars' that can be broken down into beats, half beats, quarter beats and ever-decreasing lengths of beats. The number of bars in a piece of music has no bearing on its speed; I could sing a 32-bar song quickly or slowly, but it would still be 32 bars long, in the same way that I could run a kilometre in five minutes or five hours – it would still be a kilometre. Bars are simply a system of organising music in a linear way.

You are likely to notice a recurring 'toe-tapping' rhythmic pattern in all the songs you listen to (I am referring to the rhythmic feel of the music as a whole, not specifically to what the singer is doing). Your toe is tapping to the beats in the bars, and if you listen closely you will detect an emphasis on particular beats. Although several patterns of beats are used in music, the most common can be counted in bars that last three or four beats. If you try counting out loud to a traditional waltz, you will find that you are counting in recurring bars of three beats each and there is likely to be an emphasis on beat number one. This music would be described as being 'in three' or having 'three beats in the bar'. Just as a point of interest, the term 'time signature' in music refers to the number of beats in the bar of any given piece of music. Time signatures can change during a song, sometimes for one or two bars or for the rest of the song, so if you are happily counting along and suddenly doubt yourself, it might well be that there has been a change. Trust yourself. Your instinct for the first beat of the bar is likely to be right.

All the songs you sing will have these recurring patterns; it is important to know this because if you can hear or feel the recurring first beat in the bar it should help you to stay in time with the music. You will also be able to count the number of bars in the intro, or in an instrumental break. There will be times when you will struggle with timing on a particular passage of a song. When this happens, identify the first beat of the bar and mark it up against the relevant word on your lyric sheet. As an exercise, listen to some music, both vocal and non-vocal, and see if you can count along with the bars.

Preparing your body to sing

It's good to get into the habit of preparing your body for singing before you open your mouth. This spot-check list should be helpful.

1   Check your posture (page 73): long neck, shoulders gently back and down, sternum lifted and tail bone tucked under.

2   Breath control (page 88): take a moment to establish a sense of low breathing.

3   Breath support (page 89): remind yourself of how it feels to engage your abdominal muscles for singing by placing your hands on your waist, thumbs forward, and pressing into your oblique muscles, and releasing a few sustained breaths on TSS followed by the voiced fricative, VV.

4   Relax your jaw.

Using your karaoke backing track, sing the entire song without the words, using the VV fricative to establish a connection between your voice and your abdominals. This is a fantastic way to warm up your voice and allows you to get a sense of the requirements of the music without being distracted by the words or emotions. It's worth doing this a few times. Remember not to push the air out of your mouth, but instead to 'allow' the breath to be released. You will know if you are pushing, as your voice will feel and sound unstable.

If you are struggling with higher notes, remember to stabilise your ribcage by lifting your sternum and pulling your shoulders back and down, or by squeezing the juice out of imaginary oranges held in your armpits. Bear in mind that higher notes require less air.

Preparing the vocal tract to sing the words

You will need to shape your vocal tract to a position that will feel comfortable and be appropriate for the style and emotion of the song you are about to sing. This is really important to do, or you will struggle to find resonance. Without it, your singing will sound dry and forced.

As a starting point, I would suggest that if you are singing a contemporary song (as opposed to classical) you begin by saying 'yeah' (ee-yeh) or 'meow' (without articulating the w, so it sounds like 'mee-yah'), keeping the tip of your tongue behind your bottom front teeth and dropping your jaw on the second syllable. Your tongue might feel 'wide'. You should get a resonant, twangy quality. Most importantly, the back of your tongue has come forward out of the throat, which is creating airspace behind it. The back of the mouth space should generally feel high and forward. Say each of the words several times to properly understand the sensations I am describing. Everyone feels things differently, so you may need to spend a bit of time experimenting. Learn to take this shape into your singing. (Note that preparation for classical singing involves a lower tongue, a highly arched soft palate and a more 'dome-like' space at the back of the throat. Almost the opposite to what we are aiming for in other genres.)

Now sing the words of your song with the vocal-tract shaping you have just worked on. Start by singing one phrase really, really slowly, without the music. The trick is to maintain a position that doesn't allow the tongue to go back towards the throat, which will impede the airflow and possibly create tension in the vocal tract. This takes a lot of concentration. Remember to relax your jaw, keeping a space between the upper and lower molars, and experiment with opening your mouth for different words or vowel sounds. It's not possible to produce resonance if you keep your mouth too closed or don't change the width of your jaw opening to accommodate the demands of different vowel sounds.

Adding artistry

When you feel that you have created an environment in your mouth and throat that feels comfortable for singing, you should refer to your mood board (page 134). Put the descriptive words in front of you and start to engage with the emotional context of what you are singing about (sentimental, fed-up, angry, hurt, excited, etc). You should feel this subtly but definitely, manifesting in your throat.

In music, the word 'dynamics' refers to increases and decreases in volume. In the same way that mood in speech is nuanced by shifts in volume, the same applies in singing. In classical music and musical theatre, composers often mark the shifts in dynamics on the sheet music to guide the singer and instrumentalists, but in commercial music the performer is normally expected to produce their own interpretation of the text.

Experiment with dynamics by choosing particular moments to change volume in your song. This can happen gradually through a phrase, or you might switch dynamics in blocks – when a quiet verse is followed by a rousing chorus that might warrant a gear change, for example. You can also use dynamics in just one word: if you have a long note at the end of a phrase you could start quietly and get louder, or vice versa. Extreme, sudden changes in dynamics can be very effective. Get creative.

It can be useful to imagine the words travelling forward out of your throat to a spot in front of you. This helps to avoid 'reaching up' for high notes or 'dropping' the low ones back down the throat, both of which can create stress in the larynx. Additionally, imagining a steady

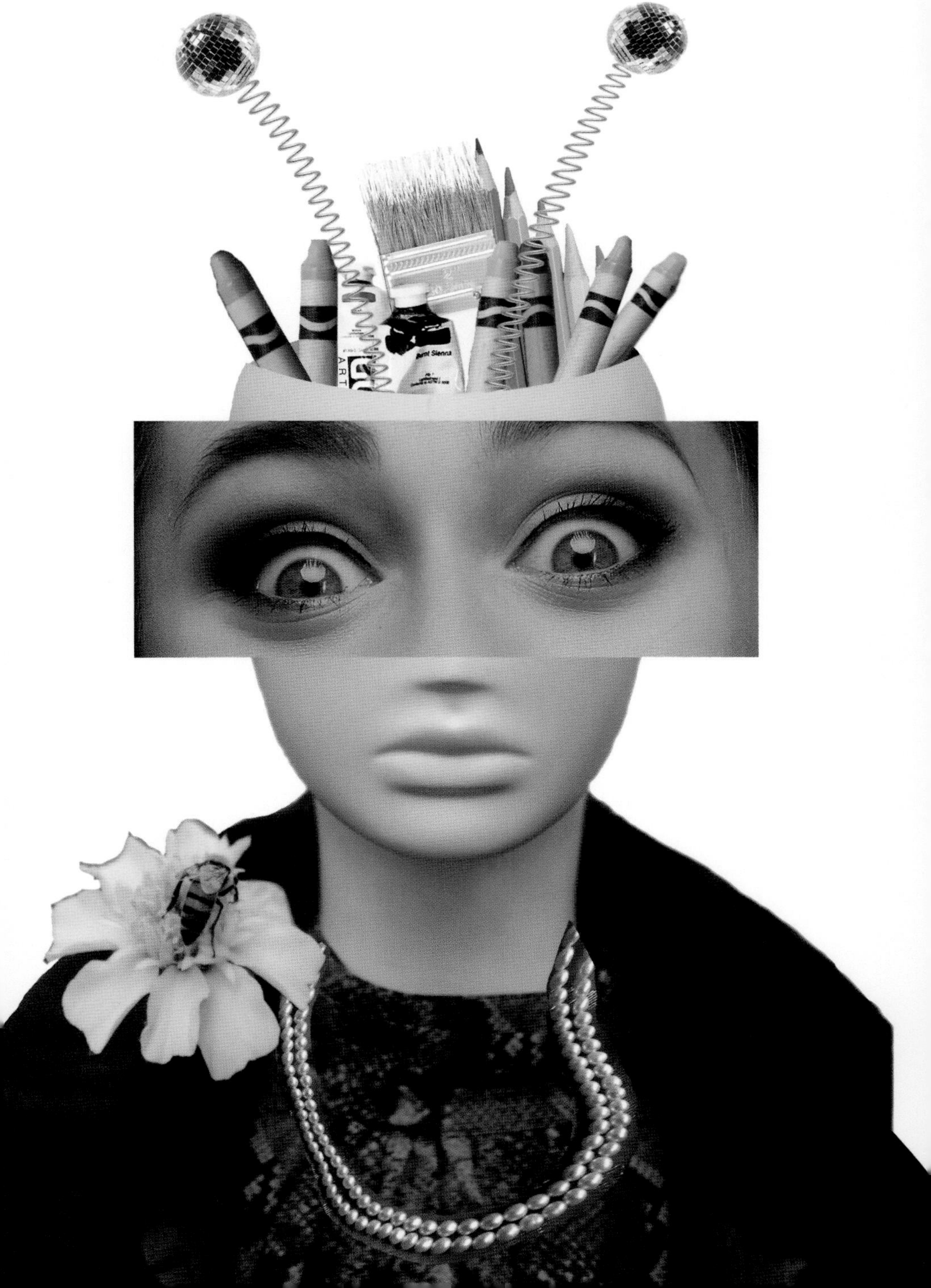
ART
Sienna

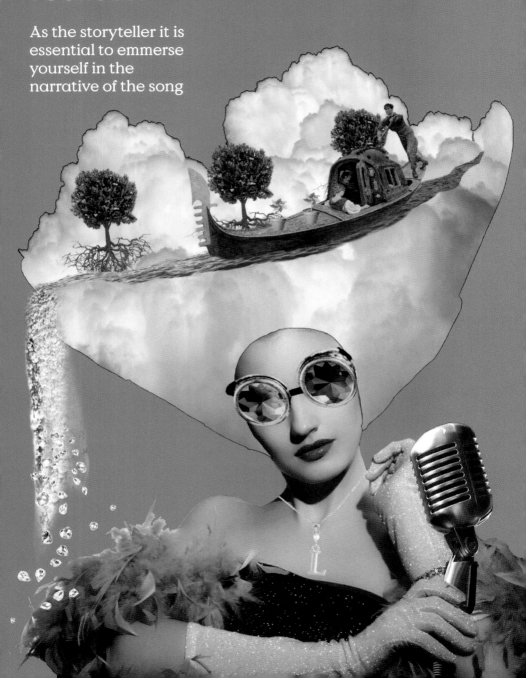

PICTURE
YOURSELF

As the storyteller it is
essential to emmerse
yourself in the
narrative of the song

flow of sound will help you to sing in smoother phrases, as opposed
to individual words that lack any connection. Stretch your arm out in
front of you, with your fingers reaching forward and keep the sound
running over your fingertips to your spot in the distance. This exercise
is about directing the sound forward and should not be confused with
increasing your volume to be heard from a distance.

Energising the beginning of each phrase is an incredibly effective
tool in conveying the meaning of text. I strongly encourage you to
invest some time on developing this skill. This sense of energy is pretty
nuanced but could be interpreted as a feeling of excitement in the
chest and throat and not related to increasing the volume. Using
commas and full stops as markers for a renewal of energy will give you
a dynamic performance. Start experimenting by imagining that you
have just been given some fantastic news and apply that feeling of
excitement in your throat to the beginning of all your phrases.

All these tips will help you deliver a song effectively. There are lots more
tools available to you to add light, shade, texture and colour to your
performance, but start by using these basic ideas and you should get
some well-earned creative satisfaction.

Learning a song in three steps

I would like to demonstrate using the uncomplicated tune and text
of Down in the River to Pray. If you are not already familiar with this
traditional American song, have a listen to Alison Krauss, whose
version was featured in the film O Brother, Where Art Thou? Although
the exact origins are unknown, the song was first published in the 1880s
and could be described variously as an African-American spiritual, a
southern gospel song or Christian folk. It is a firm favourite with close-
harmony groups.

EMOJIS

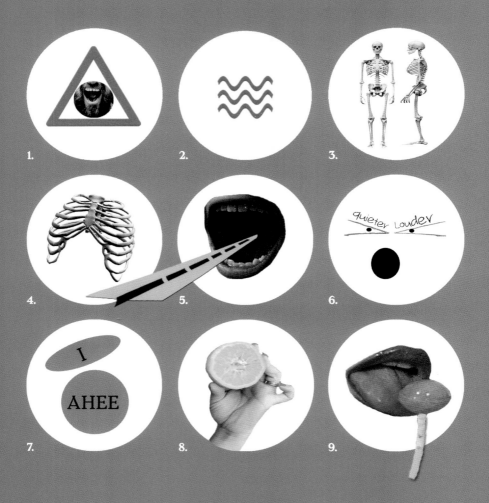

1. Don't sing loudly

2. Stretching a few vowels will let your voice ring

3. Maintain appropriate posture

4. Keep the sternum lifted

5. Imagine directing the sound to a spot in front of you - especially high and low notes

6. Vary your volume by using dynamics through phrases and words

7. You will need to change the way you shape some vowels at certain pitches

8. Squeeze the juice out of oranges in your armpits for extra stability

9. Licking a lolly will bring the back of the tongue forward and drop the jaw

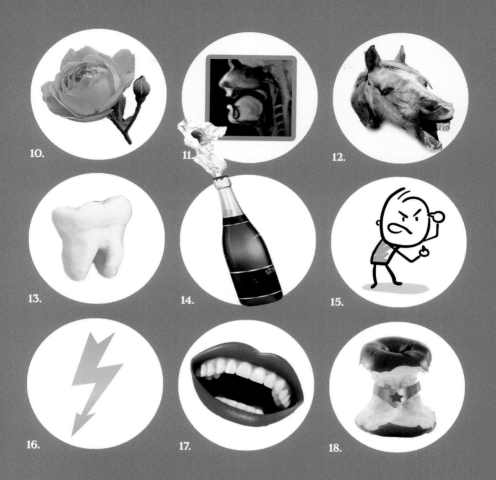

10. Imagine sniffing a rose to brighten the sound

11. Always keep space behind the tongue to let the voice ring

12. Sticking your teeth out can result in some great changes in your sound

13. A gap between your molars will relax the jaw and increase the acoustic space

14. Energise your singing - imagine the fizzy release of a champagne cork

15. A sense of complaining in your throat will help with high notes

16. Energise the beginning of every phrase

17. Laughing releases tension and lifts the back of the throat - great for high notes

18. Keep your core engaged to the end of each phrase

Step 1

Stabilising the breath and the body

• Print the lyrics of whichever song you have chosen and get familiar with how the tune goes by gently singing or humming along with a recording. Use arrows to help you remember where it goes up or down.

• Once you are familiar with your song, read the words out loud and make sense of the text.

• Mark the breaths in where they suit you – the song that I have chosen here could be sung at any speed which will make a difference to how many breaths you will need – never breathe in the middle of a word.

• Make sure that your sternum is lifted and that your jaw is relaxed and that there is space between your molars.

• Sing through the song using VV instead of words, to establish a connection between the breath and the body.

• Check that your core muscles are engaged while you sing by pushing your fingers into your waist or anywhere along the abdominal wall.

• Now sing the words, but don't sing loudly!

As I went down in the river to pray
Studying about that good old way
And who shall wear the starry crown
Good Lord show me the way!
O sisters let's go down,
Let's go down come on down,
O sisters let's go down,
Down in the river to pray.

Breath

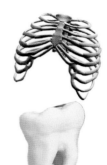

As I went down in the river to pray
Studying about that good old way
And who shall wear the robe and crown
Good Lord, show me the way!
O mothers let's go down,
Come on down, don't you want to go down,
Come on mothers, let's go down,
Down in the river to pray.

As I went down in the river to pray
Studying about that good old way
And who shall wear the starry crown
Good Lord, show me the way!
O sinners let's go down,
Let's go down, come on down,
O sinners let's go down,
Down in the river to pray.

Step 2

Vowels and tongue position

- Maintaining the ideas from Step 1, you will now need to consider your tongue position so look at the MRI scan and try to create space behind the tongue for the air to flow through.

- Imagine you are about to lick a lolly – feel your jaw drop and the back of your tongue coming forward.

- Try singing a few phrases with a finger placed between your molars – making sure you are opening your mouth sufficiently.

- Some vowels are difficult to sing at certain pitches, so I have made some suggestions for where you might experiment with changing 'OH' and 'UU' sounds to 'AH' which will allow the voice to ring and should be more comfortable to sing.

- Experiment with stretching some of the vowels, for example, on the word 'way' make the 'a' last a bit longer before you hit the 'y' or experiment with 'crown' waiting for the last second to add the 'wn'.

- Stabilise the body by squeezing the juice out of imaginary oranges in your armpits.

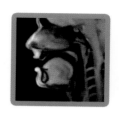

As I went down in the river to pray
Studying about that good old way
And who shall wear the starry crown
Good Lord, show me the way!
O sisters let's go down,
Let's go down, come on down,
O sisters let's go down,
Down in the river to pray.

As I went down in the river to pray
Studying about that good old way
And who shall wear the robe and crown
Good Lord, show me the way!
O mothers let's go down,
Come on down, don't you want to go down,
Come on mothers, let's go down,
Down in the river to pray.

As I went down in the river to pray
Studying about that good old way
And who shall wear the starry crown
Good Lord, show me the way!
O sinners let's go down,
Let's go down, come on down,
O sinners let's go down,
Down in the river to pray.

AH

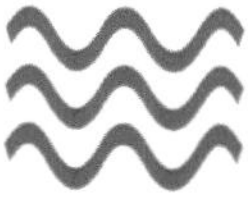

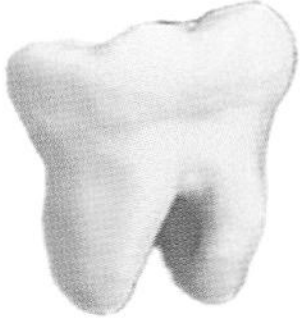

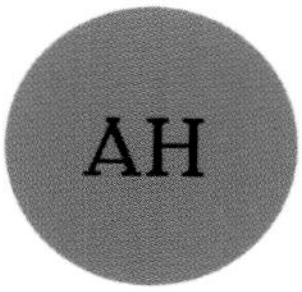

Step 3

Artistry and performance

- Imagining that you are directing (not pushing) your sound to a spot in front of you will give you smoother phrasing and stop you from reaching up for high notes or pushing down for low ones.

- Energising the beginning of each phrase is a brilliant way to help convey the meaning of the words – this does not mean getting louder!

- Imagine the energy behind a popping champagne cork - it's that!

- Try laughing as you sing, keeping that sense of relaxation in the throat throughout.

- Add dynamics – getting louder or softer through a phrase or in a single word and then try an entire line quietly and another line with increased volume. Thinking about the words as you sing them will create a natural flow of dynamics. Never sing at the same volume all the way through a song.

- Experiment with changing the quality of the sound – stick your upper teeth out like a horse or try sniffing the flower. Perhaps pout your lips and sing breathily and then with more twang.

- Get artistic!

As I went down in the river to pray
Studying about that good old way
And who shall wear the starry crown
Good Lord, show me the way!
O sisters let's go down,
Let's go down, come on down,
O sisters let's go down,
Down in the river to pray.

As I went down in the river to pray
Studying about that good old way
And who shall wear the robe and crown
Good Lord, show me the way!
O mothers let's go down,
Come on down, don't you want to go down,
Come on mothers, let's go down,
Down in the river to pray.

As I went down in the river to pray
Studying about that good old way
And who shall wear the starry crown
Good Lord, show me the way!
O sinners let's go down,
Let's go down, come on down,
O sinners let's go down,
Down in the river to pray.

quieter louder

CHAPTER TWELVE

DIFFERENT STYLES, DIFFERENT RULES

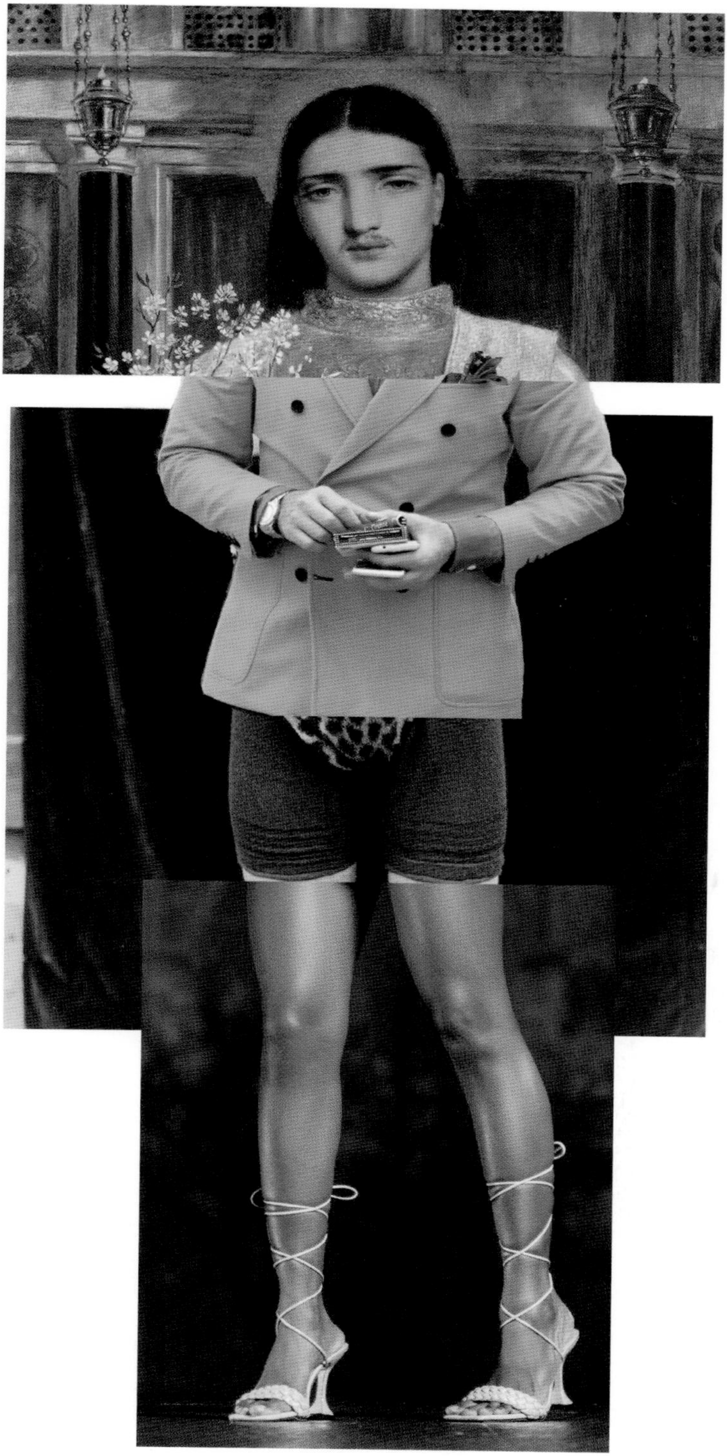

Different styles, different rules

Every genre has its own requirements

While the rules of singing technique are fundamental, different genres have their own artistic requirements. If you are keen to look at jazz repertoire, for example, you will need to focus more on rhythm and phrasing than someone who might want to go down the classical route. Whatever style you choose, there will be requirements to consider before you approach the music.

In **classical music** the singer is normally required to perform exactly what the composer has written. This is a bit of a generalisation, as there are many, many forms of classical music, but it is a good rule to follow if you are dipping your toe in for the first time.

The classical sound is 'round', dark and rich in resonance, and produced by arching the soft palate to create the sensation of a large space in the throat behind the tongue, and in the mouth. A smooth quality (called legato), created by emphasising the vowels (among other things), and a pronounced vibrato, are distinguishing features in classical singing. The singer relies on technical strategies to be able to deliver nuanced performances that can still be heard above an orchestra without requiring a microphone.

Unlike most classical performances, **musical theatre** is generally amplified with microphones, which means the singer doesn't have to work to project in the same way that a classical singer does. So, in contrast to the high-arched soft palate employed in classical singing, the musical-theatre performer is likely to use a flatter, smaller mouth shape with a less pronounced vibrato. The words are extremely important and the use of consonants more pronounced. A degree of creative freedom with phrasing is allowed to help express the emotional highs and lows. There are some musicals, including Phantom of the Opera and Carousel, in which the singing style shares some stylistic qualities with classical singing: this is called **legit singing**. The term legit is short for 'legitimate', but that does not mean other musical-theatre styles are 'illegitimate' or inferior in any way. These days, musicals include all kinds of styles of music, many of which are shared with contemporary commercial genres (pop, rock, country and so on).

Musical-theatre singing, by its very nature, requires the singer to be able to 'act' or embody the character they are playing, including maintaining the qualities of their character's speaking voice through to their singing voice and to fully understand their role in the wider story. Acknowledging context, circumstance and character is therefore absolutely essential.

If you are going to be singing a musical-theatre song as a standalone number, as jazz singers often do, you are no longer constrained by the implications of the wider story and the context can become whatever you decide to make it. Think of Gershwin's 'Summertime' from Porgy and Bess, or Rodgers and Hart's 'The Lady is a Tramp' from Babes in Arms, which have been covered by hundreds of artists to the point where the concepts of the original settings are lost. The fabulous jazz singer Ella Fitzgerald famously transformed Cole Porter's musical songs into standalone jazz songs that are still considered to be a vital part of every jazz singer's repertoire.

It is almost a requirement of jazz not to sing what's written! Jazz sheet music is often presented as a skeleton of vital information, known as a 'lead sheet', allowing the musicians to improvise with freedom. The singer needs to understand the structure of the song and be prepared to lead the band, often using a system of hand signals to indicate tempo (speed) and key changes and to give structural shape to the song. Jazz encompasses many kinds of musical forms, including latin, swing, bebop and fusion, all of which are centred on rhythm.

Commercial music is open to any kind of interpretation. These songs can be put into a key that suits the voice of the individual singer and it is acceptable to change a few notes or rewrite words to fit the gender or personal statement of the performer. It is also common for people to create their own arrangements of commercial songs; an 'arrangement' takes into account the type of musical instruments used and how they are used, as well as modifications to the structure, speed and feel of the rhythm. You might choose to sing a song slowly with a sparse piano accompaniment or with an orchestra of dustbin lids and tubular bells, whereas the original performer might have had a faster arrangement that included strings or brass sections. Commercial singing uses a variety of different voice qualities, including twangy, breathy, speech-quality and clear tone, all four of which are achieved by making a small, flat space at the back of your mouth.

As an exercise, try a variety of styles that you might not feel naturally connected to. You might be surprised by how well you sing.

CHAPTER THIRTEEN

EASY MISTAKES TO MAKE

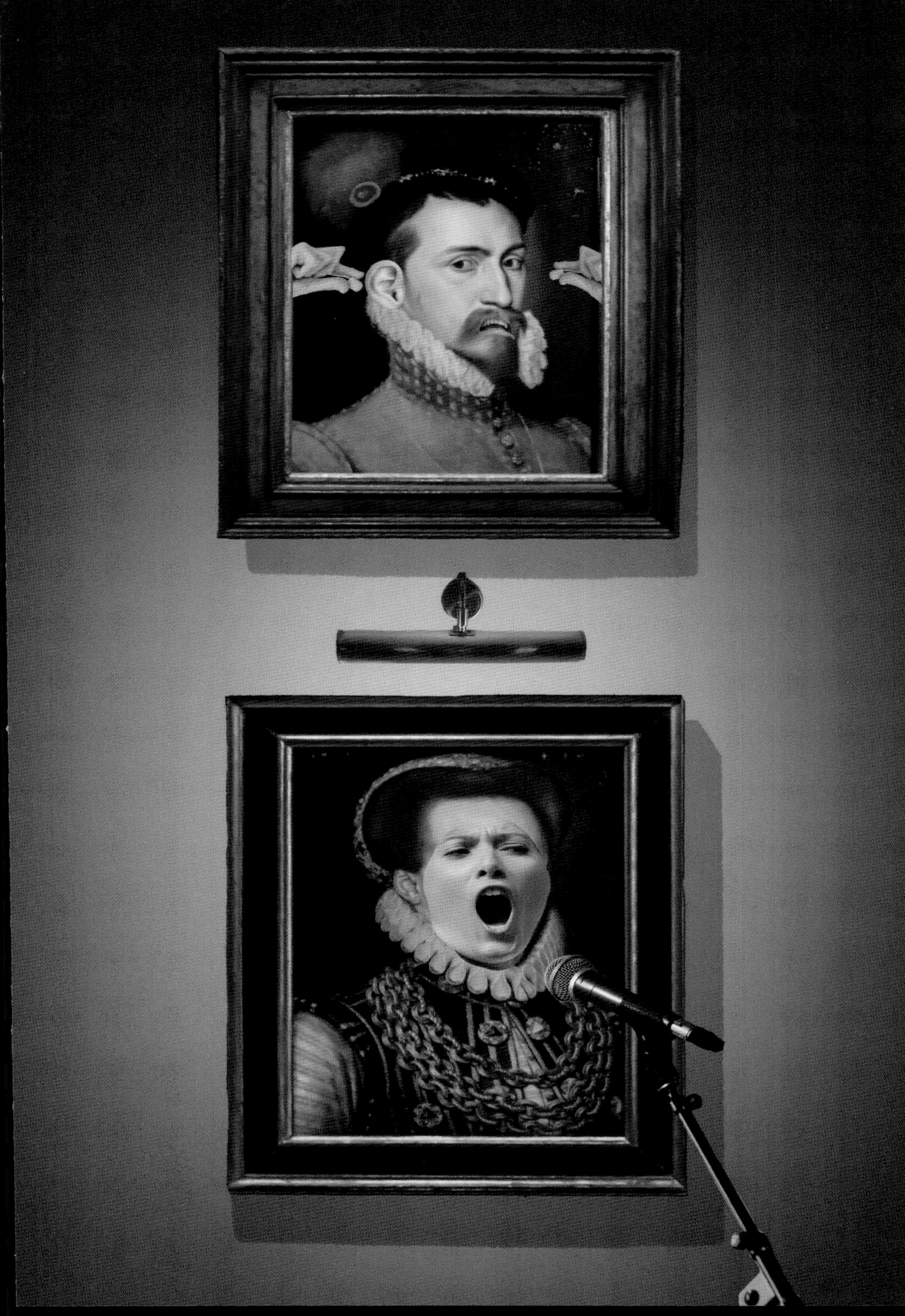

Easy mistakes to make

Pushing and straining in the throat is the most common and understandable mistake of them all

It is only by making mistakes that we learn, and learning from other people's mistakes is as good a way as any! Please don't be daunted by this list; I have included just about everything I can think of that every singer will do at some point. Always bear in mind that everyone stumbles while developing new skills and that nobody is judging you. You have done so well to get to this point. I am a great believer in 'negative' practice, so if you and I were in the studio together I would ask you to feel the right and wrong way to do things. I would suggest you try this for yourself when dealing with some of the following.

- **Using too much effort** The most common and understandable mistake of them all! Pushing and straining in the throat is always detrimental to the quality of the sound and can result in fatigue and hoarseness. You will soon come to understand that many of the problems faced by singers are caused by using too much effort. Trust yourself; it is perfectly possible to sing with very little effort if you follow the rules that you have you learned in this book. Use your abdominal support muscles to stabilise your voice and allow your larynx to be free to do what it needs to do.

- **Not warming up** You may not feel like it; you may want to just get on with the actual singing – but warming up matters! Warm muscles work more efficiently and productively than cold ones.

Try warming up thoroughly one day and then singing with cold muscles on another day and see how each feels.

- **Singing with a closed mouth** This is so unbelievably common and can greatly impact the quality of the sound. Often singers can't feel when their mouths are closed, so it's worth looking in a mirror and observing how wide you are opening your mouth while singing. A small, closed jaw space will rob you of resonance and feel uncomfortable when you're singing in your higher ranges. If in doubt, place a finger between your back teeth and keep it there while singing. If you find that you are biting on your finger, you are probably singing with a tight jaw. A singer's jaw position is continually changing depending on the vowel and the pitch.

- **Singing too loudly** Sustained loud singing is vocally tiring and ultimately rather boring to listen to, so save it for the occasional dynamic in a song when the lyric really warrants it. You will also find that quieter singing feels more comfortable.

- **Singing out of tune** Go easy on yourself with this. I have taught singers who started out not being able to sing a note in tune and whose ability to improve simply came through practising the core principles of technique. Singing out of tune does not signify a lack of ability; it can be a result of poor core muscle stability, singing too loudly, straining in the throat and lack of practice. There are numerous tuning apps available for tablets and phones which can be very helpful if you are not sure if you are singing in tune.

- **Running out of air** Please refer to Troubleshooting your breath control (page 104).

- **Jaw and tongue tension** Singing with a small or tight jaw not only robs you of resonance (as I have described above) but can introduce tension into the joint (which is called the temporomandibular joint). Tension in your tongue will also impact the quality of the sound: tension can drive a stiff tongue backward down your throat, impeding airflow and resonance. Warm your tongue up with stretches and trills (page 109) before singing and make a conscious effort to keep the back of it, high and forward. Resting a straw or pencil across your bottom lip and along your lower teeth, and then singing with your tongue hanging out over the top of the straw, may make articulation very difficult, but will remind you of how it feels to have a forward-placed, high tongue.

- **Sounding nasal** If your singing sounds too nasal, pay attention to your soft palate (page 46). The soft palate is the gateway to your nose: if the gateway is left open, the sound will travel out through your nose, giving your singing a nasal quality, and if it is closed, the sound will be diverted out of your mouth.

- **Singing at the same volume all the way through a song** No matter how subtle, every song should include waves of volume. Even if there are no immediately obvious places to sing a dynamic (page 138), you can still include swells through long notes or build up or down through phrases.

- **Straining to reach high notes** The science shows us that our vocal folds get thinner and longer as the pitch of what we are singing gets higher, and that this stretching can only be achieved by the free movement of the larynx. Straining to reach high notes introduces stress into the vocal tract and interferes with this free movement, thus preventing the vocal cords from stretching as they need to. There should be no unwanted tension in the vocal tract during singing. Appropriate relaxation can be achieved by laughing, silently or audibly; additionally, imagining yourself whingeing or moaning can coax the larynx into a position that makes reaching the high notes much easier. Experiment with the amount of air you are using and see how singing with less air, which may feel like you are singing quietly, might feel easier.

- **Sounding more like you are speaking than singing** If you need to add musicality to your singing, stretching a few vowels would be the first step. It is the vowels that ring in your vocal tract, producing lots of lovely harmonics; the consonants are there to make words out of vowels. Try stretching your vowels in a few phrases and see the immediate difference. If you are feeling a bit unsure about this, have a listen to Frank Sinatra, whose way with vowel sounds is what makes him the king of phrasing. He definitely did do it His Way!

- **Not practising** Yep! Singing is a muscular and intellectual activity and like any other, needs to be practised. You will always find it difficult to coordinate your body if you don't practise. But trust me, what feels unnatural to start with will become second nature with enough repetition.

- **Unfocused practising** Singing a song over and over again in the same way will not make you sing it any better, and it will be disheartening. Choose one or two things to focus on when you practise and your learning will be faster and more satisfying.

CHAPTER

FOURTEEN

THE

NEXT

STEP

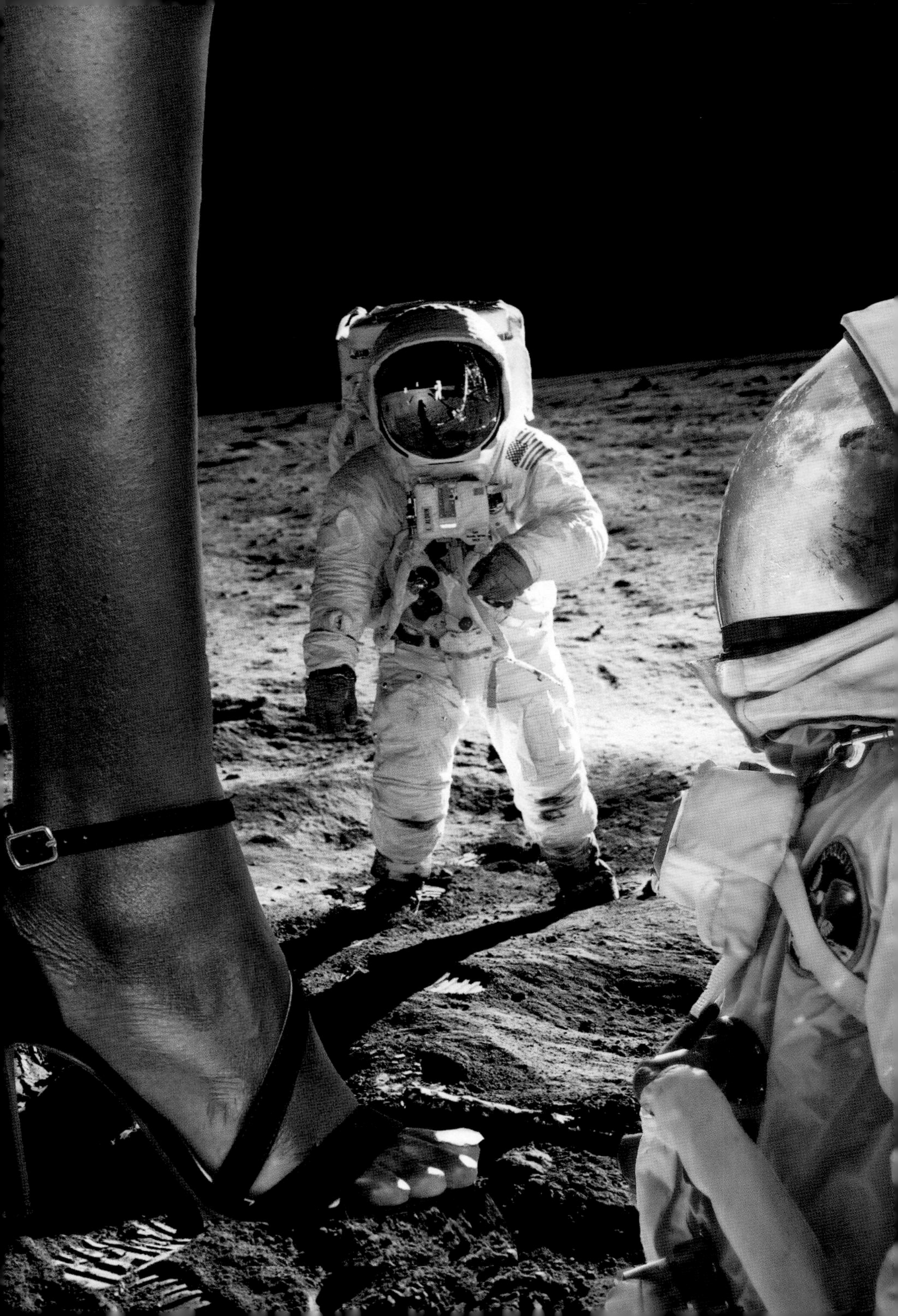

The next step

Whatever the circumstances, you can sing yourself proud by focusing your mind on your technique

If you have successfully navigated your way through the core disciplines of singing described in this book, congratulations!

Hopefully you will be delighted with what you have achieved. As you proceed on your singing journey, there will be days when you find you can't sing as well as the day before. Don't be discouraged; that is the nature of the living instrument. Our bodies are constantly changing. Our voices are affected by hormones, diet, sleep, hydration, anxiety and depression, and undergo a perpetual natural evolution with age. Challenging moments can arise at any time, so if you face a hitch, be ready to step back and leave it for a day or two, or self-diagnose and explore what you can do to help yourself without getting stressed. Bear in mind, too, that you need to keep using your voice regularly to keep it in shape, so if you have a few weeks off, be gentle on yourself and don't expect to necessarily be able to pick up where you left off. Keep this little book handy to remind yourself of the basics.

Once you've gained some confidence, you may want to take things further. A few sessions with a singing teacher will make a big difference, as long as you practise between lessons. However, finding the right teacher to match your needs and personality can be a bit daunting, so I hope the following goes some way towards helping you make the right decision.

Ten things to consider when looking for a singing teacher

1 **Qualifications** Singing teaching (in the UK) is unregulated and there are no compulsory teaching qualifications. Don't be embarrassed to ask about the nature of a prospective teacher's experience and to draw your own conclusions. Bear in mind that a first-class degree in music, majoring in piano with a module on singing, is an impressive achievement but not a qualification to teach singing.

2 **Setting goals** Set yourself some goals, no matter how loose (perhaps you'd like to join a choir, improve the quality of your tone, increase your range or learn a particular song), to give yourself a focus for what you want from singing lessons. Most singing teachers want to be matched to the right student as much as that student wants to find the best teacher for their needs, so it's really helpful to share your objectives.

3 **Continuing professional development** Vocal science and research is ongoing and a teacher who invests in their professional development by attending seminars and masterclasses, and by connecting with other practitioners, will add value to your lessons. A teacher who is engaged in this way will be more than happy to tell you about it, so ask them.

4 **Professional standing** A reputable singing teacher (in the UK) is likely to belong to professional organisations such as the British Voice Association, the Association of Teachers of Singing (AOTOS) or the Musicians' Union.

5 **Personality** You may well feel self-conscious and vulnerable the first time you sing for a teacher, so it's important to find someone that you like and feel safe with. You'll know.

6   **Genre or style** There are singing teachers who specialise in particular styles of singing, so if you already know that you want to specifically learn metal or opera or beatboxing, ask them if they teach that style. There are also terrific 'general' teachers who will be able to help you develop technique and musicality and who successfully teach in a range of styles.

7   **Try before you buy** No matter how tempted you are by a 'bulk buy' offer, don't commit to lots of classes without trying a few sessions first.

8   **Pace yourself – and practise** If you commit to weekly lessons but find that you don't have time to practise in between, reduce the sessions to every two or three weeks. Learning to sing must never become a chore. It is perfectly possible to progress with fortnightly sessions as long as you commit to practise. Your teacher is there to facilitate your learning, but ultimately it's up to you to put the time in.

9   **The right songs** The songs you sing should be ones that you connect with, that suit your goals and that are right for your level of skill. For a singing teacher, finding the right repertoire for a new student can be challenging and may take a few attempts, so give them as much information about your likes, dislikes and musical tastes as possible, while remaining open to trying new things. Don't stick with songs you really don't like – but don't give up on songs just because they feel too hard. You need to have faith in your teacher's assessment of your capabilities.

10   **Moving on** As a singing teacher, I occasionally get students that I think would be better served by a different teacher. In these cases I am happy to make recommendations. If you feel that the relationship isn't quite right for you, don't be afraid to have an open conversation with your teacher, who might well agree and help you find a better way forward.

From the singing teacher's point of view

When asked which teaching 'method' I ascribe to, I normally answer with a rather convoluted ramble about how there is no 'one-size fits all' approach to singing teaching, as each voice is unique to the individual and subject to an infinite number of variables. It is, however, a perfectly obvious line of enquiry from prospective new students – after all, there are prescribed methods of teaching other instruments. The big difference, though, is that unlike other acoustic musical instruments the vocal tract is a living organism and can change shape radically. It would take a lifetime of study for any single teacher to fully learn and understand all the physical, neurological and psychological variables of voice production. So, as teachers we are always evaluating and responding to the individual needs of the voices we are working with.

And finally – learn to trust yourself

I would like to leave you with this anecdote.

I have been one of a busy cabaret duo called ShooShooBaby for many years. One of our early bookings was to perform a musical Christmas cabaret for the senior board members of a large corporation. Our regular pianist wasn't available for the job and his replacement managed to get drunk between the rehearsal and the performance. Meanwhile, explosions of whooping, applause and male heckling could be heard coming from the dining room, where we were soon to be performing, before the door was flung open and two completely naked ladies came rushing out. It became chillingly clear that our sweet, melodious, fully clothed act had been booked to perform immediately after a pair of Stripping Santas.

As we began our first song, the drunken pianist knocked his music off the piano, which drew a cheer from the mob. Regardless, he carried

SHOOSHOOBABY

Me on the right

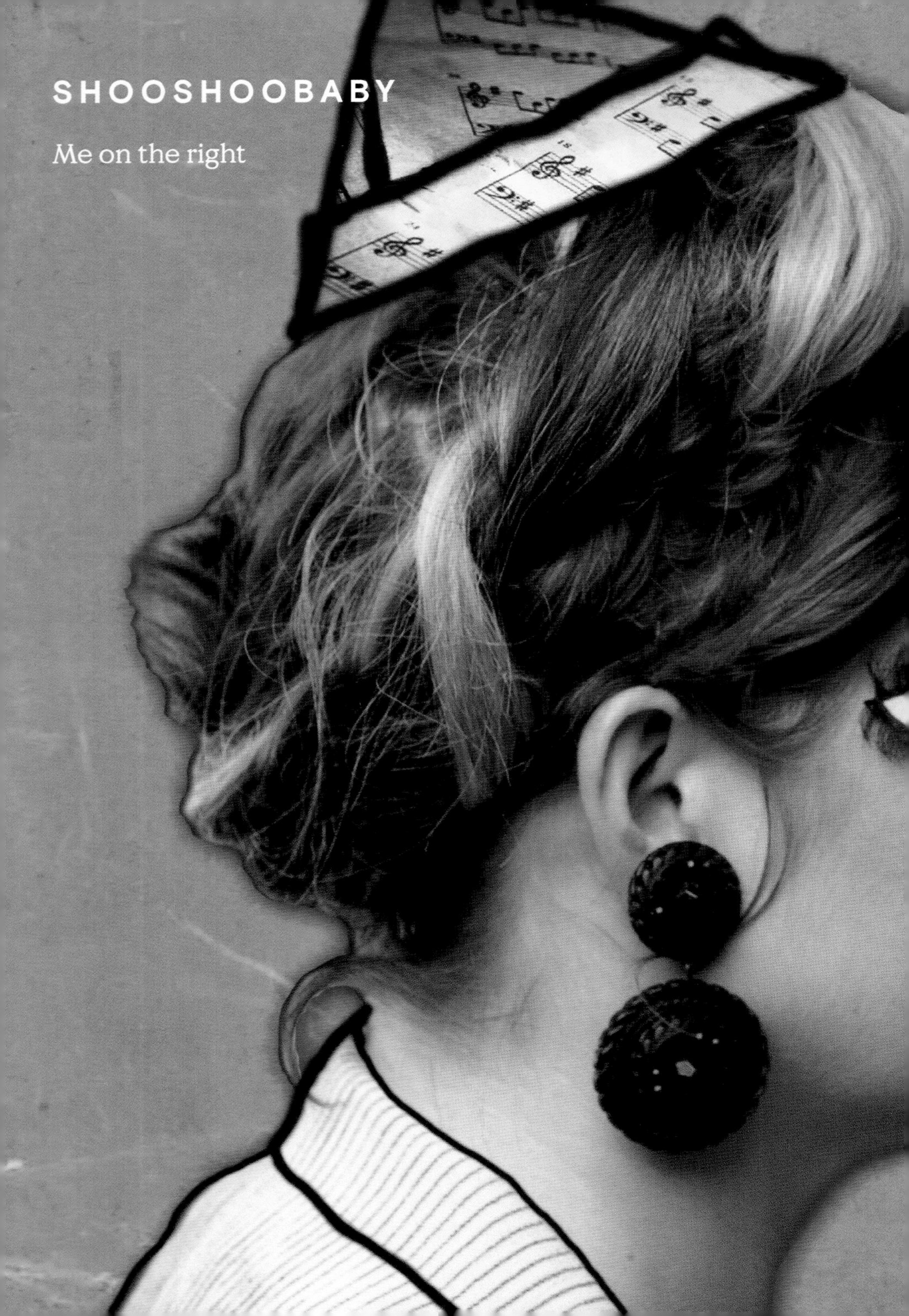

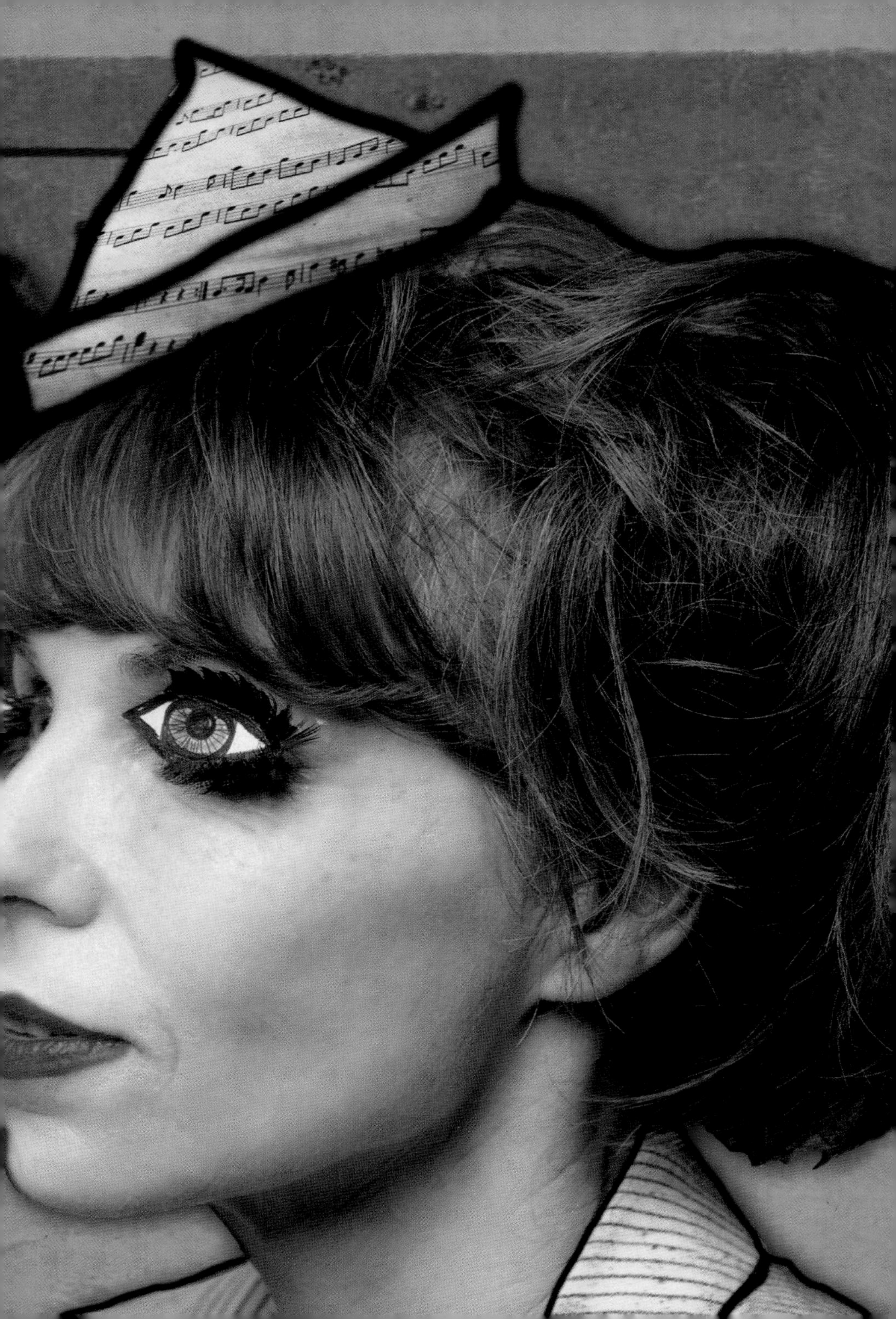

on playing as if it was still in front of him, improvising his way through an invisible score. My partner, Anna Braithwaite, valiantly carried on singing through the increasingly loud cacophony of heckling, while I, for reasons I still don't quite understand, sat myself provocatively on a man's lap. From that moment we lost control. I sang terribly and the audience understandably had no idea if we were strippers or comedians. I was traumatised by this experience but recognised that it taught me some invaluable lessons: to trust my myself as a singer, to stick to what I do best and that trying too hard to please an audience can have the opposite effect.

I have had many other 'character building' experiences in my professional life as a singer – including having a jacket potato lobbed at me. In an interactive moment on a cruise ship I attempted to shake the hand of someone who, it transpired, had passed away during the show. Obviously not a reflection on the quality of the performance! On a handful of occasions I have had to abandon malfunctioning microphones and sing acoustically. Every time, no matter how big the audience, venue or challenge, I have breathed low, engaged my core muscles, squeezed the juice out of the imaginary oranges in my armpits and pulled off a good performance.

If, further down the line, you find yourself in a situation where your nerves get the better of you – singing in front of your family or at an open-mic night or a karaoke event where the audience is chatting and not acknowledging you, for example – just remember that you can sing yourself proud by focusing your mind on your technique. Trust yourself and your voice will work for you. Don't change the song you have prepared at the last minute because you think the audience might not like it. Don't resort to closing your eyes and exaggerating the emotional narrative to win an audience over or to distract them from shaky singing – that never works. Just keep practising regularly and don't forget what you have learned in this book.

NOW

SING

!

Glossary

Abdominals The muscles of the wall of the abdominal cavity, including the external and internal obliques and the transverse and rectus abdominis

Articulators The parts of the mouth, including the lips, tongue and teeth, that we use to create words and sounds

Breath support Using the core muscles to stabilise the body for singing

Core The muscles of the body's midsection: front, back and sides

Diaphragm The dome-shaped muscle, separating the chest cavity from the abdominal cavity, that is responsible for drawing air into the lungs

Dynamics A term relating to varying volume in singing

Falsetto A soft, breathy style of high singing often used by choir boys and popular in contemporary singing; the term is also used to describe forms of female singing in classical music

Hyoid bone The horseshoe-shaped bone at the top of the larynx

Larynx Another word for the **voice box**, the larynx is a cartilaginous tube that houses the vocal folds and can be seen moving up and down during swallowing

Lateral muscles (musculus latissimus dorsi) The powerful muscles of the back

Legato Smooth and connected singing

Oblique muscles The outermost of the abdominal muscles, sometimes described as the muscles of the waist

Pharynx The region above the larynx at the back of the throat

Reflux A back flow of digestive juices into the throat that causes inflammation and severe irritation

Resonance Intensity of acoustic energy in the vocal tract

Resonating space An airspace through which vibrating air is turned into sound

Siren Gentle glides through ranges of notes, applied to warm up the voice and extend range

Soft palate The spongey back portion of the roof of the mouth that serves as the gateway to the nose

Staccato Very short, light and disconnected notes in singing; the opposite of legato

Sternum The breastbone in the centre of the ribcage, to which the ribs are attached

Trill Alternating notes, produced very quickly

Vibrato An intentional stylised wobble in the voice, used as an effect in many styles of music, most notably in classical singing

Vocal cords/folds Two muscular folds in the larynx, through which air passes to create vibration for sound

Vocal tract The resonating spaces through which vibrating air passes from the vocal folds all the way to the lips and nostrils

Voice box See **larynx**

Collage Credits

All collages created by ©Tanya Holt, protected under UK and International Copyright. Sharing or copying of any sort is illegal.

Posters and postcards are available to purchase through:
www.tooembarrassedtosing.com

Additional credits:

Too Embarrassed To Sing & Portrait of an Embarrassed Lady 1570s England. Artist uncertain (introduction).

Marble Heads Library images.

Spot the Difference Additional hand drawing Dotty Holt, 16th century image – illustrator unidentified.

The Kitchen Singer Photographers: Sincerely Media, istock, Shutterstock.

The Shower Singer Photographers: Timothy Dykes, stock images.

Lettuce & Larynx Main photograph: Jessica Felicio.

Air Flow Photographs: Jonathan Borba, Robert Lukeman, David Clode.

Beautiful Man Holding Larynx Photographs: Norbert Buduczki (main image), Jennifer Marquez, Lobostudio Hamburg, istock.

Larynx Detail Illustrations Library images.

Getting to Know Your Vocal Tract Library images.

Mouth Illustration Library image.

Tongues Painting: The Company of Captain Pieter Dircksz Hasselaer and Lieutenant Jan Gerritsz Hooft, Amsterdam c. 1595-1605 Rijksmuseum. Tongue photographers: Catherine Heath, Hayes Potter, Joey Nicotra, Karsten Winegeart, Victoria Krivchenkova, Old Youth.

Vowel shaping with MRIs (lots of them) All MRI images Max Planck Institute, Berlin by kind permission. Photographs: Cesar Rincon, Ellie Adams.

Mouth Shape Changes Everything (x4) Photographers: Main statue photo Lena Varzar.

Space Between the Molars Photographers: Brian McGowan, Ivan Diaz, Kevin Bation, NASA, istock.

Horses' Teeth Party Stock images.

Sniffing The Rose Main image: iStock.

Tension Is Your Enemy Main image stock.

Posture Main photograph of Anna Pavlova, New York Public LIbrary.

The Dropped Sternum Sternum Photograph Meta Zahren.

Skeletons Photographs: Julien Lavalee & iStock.

Swan's Neck Photographs: Patricia Prudente, Ralf Skirr, Raphael Renter.

Breathing For Singing Main photograph: Drew Dau.

Chest Cavity Photograph: Main photo Cristian Newman.

Xrays: Front & Side Views Xray: iStock.

Singing From The Core Photographs: Woman's face by Joshua Oyebanji, iStock.

Main Muscles Of Breath Support Photographs: iStock.

Squeezing Oranges In The Armpits Photographs: Joseph Kellner, Anthony Au.

Learning From Others Photographs: Alex Ware, David Suarez & iStock.

Vocal Health Matters Painting: Medea, 1868, Frederck Sandys courtesy of the Birmingham Museums Trust.

How To Learn And Perform A Song Photographs: iStock.

Using Artistry And Imagination In Singing Photographs: Michael van Kerckhove, Joshua Eckstein.

The Girl With Kaleidoscope Eyes / Picture Yourself The Gondola, 1868 Frederick Walker, Birmingham Museum Trust Photographs: iStock, Daniel Robert Dinu, Rafael Garcin, Simon Marsault.

Sending The Sound Forward Photographs: Kenrick Mills, Alexander Krivitskiy.

Different Styles, Different Rules Painting of saint by Simeon Solomon, 1867/68. Photographs: Boston Public Library, Mariya Georgieva, Vladimir Yelizarov.

East Mistakes to Make: Singing Too Loudly Paintings; Robert Dudley, Earl of Essex, Portrait of a Lady 1570 England. Artists uncertain. Museum of Victoria, Australia.

A Giant Step Library pictures.

ShooShooBaby Photograph James Millar, styling Suki Miles.

Author Biography

Tanya Holt is a singing teacher, singer, producer and satirical songwriter working mostly in cabaret and in musical theatre. Her self-penned song cycle Cautionary Tales for Daughters was described by The Times as 'Think Hilaire Belloc does Caitlin Moran' and 'gut-punchingly beautiful'; The Stage called it 'razor-sharp... beautifully performed'.

As a singer she is best known as one half of the cabaret duo ShooShooBaby, who have been appreciated by audiences internationally.

'What sets ShooShooBaby apart is their musical wit and superb harmony. Effortlessly funny.'
The Scotsman

Tanya began teaching singing in 2009 and continues to work with people of all ages and at all levels, from hobbyists to aspiring and established professionals. She is extremely interested in vocal science and the bio-mechanics of producing sound and a firm believer that anyone can learn how to sing well.

Based in southeast London, she lives with her cat Sir Gary and daughter Dotty. This is her first book.

ME IN
CAUTIONARY
TALES FOR
DAUGHTERS

When Sylvia's turned 40, her tow
Her head touched the clouds as s
Madmen and old knights sometin

sky blue, who's it,

7   8

Photo: Scott Wishart

Dedicated to Eileen Burke 1939 - 2020

My beautiful mother, whose support has made this book possible

Fellow professionals, friends and students who listened, advised and enabled this project: Anne Leatherland, Anna Braithwaite, David Mills, Dotty Holt, Esther Bell, James Cleeve, Juliet Evans, Lucy Mars, Mandy Burke, Robert Burke, Toby Gutmann.

I am indebted to Dr Gillyanne Kayes and Jeremy Fisher who stoked my interest in vocal science and taught me how to be an effective singing teacher – giants in their field.

Photo libraries: iStock, Shutterstock and Elements Envato and all the photographers and institutions who donate their work through unsplash.com